Novel #3 in the Mr. Right Novel Series

Marrying Mr. Right

by Lisa Raftery

and Barbara Precourt

Harrison House

Published by
Harrison House Publishing
Tulsa, OK

15 14 13 12   10 9 8 7 6 5 4 3 2 1

Marrying Mr. Right

ISBN: 978-1-160683-495-4

Copyright © 2012 by Lisa Raftery and Barbara Precourt

Published by Harrison House Publishers, Inc.

Cover Photography: Scott Miller, Miller Photography Tulsa, OK

Cover Models: Olivia Ophus and Caleb Ophus

Cover Design: Christian Ophus

Endorsements

Marrying Mr. Right is such an awesome book! I've loved all of the novels in this series, unable to put them down! I liked novel 3 because it encourages you to keep believing God, even in the difficult times when, like Julia, you're tempted to lose hope. But she kept trusting God, and that's what I'm going to do, too. This novel has so many good values as well as issues that girls like me can relate to. You're going to LOVE watching Julia fall in love with David, and the ending is great! I recommend this book to any teen wanting a great read.

Calyn Sutherland, age 16

This third novel was a perfect end to the Mr. Right Series, full of sound marital wisdom and a good dose of suspense! You will love watching Julia try to make it to the altar at last! As a parent of a 16-year-old daughter, this series has been a valuable tool for discussing issues and strengthening communication. I highly recommend it to parents who are trying to reach their teen girls, especially the more independent, spirited ones.

Krista Cobb,
Co-founder of DBA Worldwide

Wow, I am amazed by this series! *Marrying Mr. Right* does not disappoint with its engaging plot and awesome ending! Barbara and Lisa do a wonderful job teaching Biblical truths through Julia's life. It's a perfect series for young women: romantic and funny, while all along teaching the importance of purity. There is such a reward when you wait for the "Mr. Right" in your life. If girls get hold of these novels and discover that truth for themselves, I believe we will have a generation of girls saving themselves instead of giving themselves away.

Alyssa Shull
Founder of the 'Pink Lid'
Purity Conference,
Host of Skunks TV

This third novel allows you to share Julia's highs and lows in her courtship with David. It provides an honest portrayal of the dynamics involved in court-ship, including the effects of past relationships, the importance of communication, and the need for family boundaries. Regardless of your age, this novel will inspire you to honor God and reap the rewards of waiting for and then marrying Mr. Right.

Melissa Hurst, Psy.D.
Clinical Psychologist

Dedication

Marrying Mr. Right is the third novel in our daughter/mother project together. We dedicate it to each of our daughters and granddaughters:

Girls, the entire MR. RIGHT SERIES is our legacy—a written expression of our love, something of us that can be passed down to mentor and bless not only each of you, but eventually your daughters and granddaughters as well, should the Lord tarry.

Please know that we have earnestly prayed for you. We're believing each of you will come to see that becoming wives and mothers in the Kingdom of God is a worthy calling, that you will recognize the eternal importance of that call and prepare your hearts to answer it.

Acknowledgements

We want to extend our deepest gratitude to the following people who helped make this novel possible:

Stephanie Precourt, Kim Sgouroudis, Tracy Irvin, and Lisa Kondas, for their support and valuable input.

Pastors Larry & Victoria Raftery, for their prayers and constant support throughout this project.

Our husbands, Eric Raftery and Roger Precourt, for their continual love, support, and encouragement.

Most of all, our Heavenly Father, for giving us the privilege to write this series for Him.

Contents

The Shortcut

It was early morning in Jasper Falls, and many of the stores and restaurants hadn't opened yet. Even so, parking spaces were filling up as both locals and tourists began making their way into town to shop. Turning onto Main Street, I spied an open spot in front of Perkins' Jewelry Store. As I pulled in, the sign in the front window was just being flipped to read **OPEN FOR BUSINESS**.

"Perfect timing," I commented to the golden retriever comfortably stretched out on the back seat. Shifting into park, I pulled the key out of the ignition and told Sandy, "Stay here, girl. I'll be back in a few minutes." Checking to see that the windows were cracked enough to give the dog some ventilation, I grabbed my purse and headed inside.

Mr. Perkins must have seen me drive up while he was adjusting the window sign because the door opened before I could turn the knob. The elderly shopkeeper reached for my hand to greet me.

"Good morning, young lady," he said with a smile. "Kinda thought you might be droppin' by. If I'm not mistaken, your big day's almost here."

"Right, Mr. Perkins. In a few days my name will be Mrs. David Stanton. I came by to pick up the item I left with you several weeks ago. It *is* finished, I hope? I called yesterday, and your wife said you'd have it ready for me first thing this morning."

"Promised you, did she? Well, seems like she said somethin' to me about that, too. Let's take a look under the counter over here," he added, winking at me. Slowly, he shuffled his way across the room. Bending down, he pulled out a box from a drawer beneath the display case. "Yep, here she is, all shined up and ready to give to your fiancé."

Excited, I took the box from the kindly gentleman and opened it. Tucked neatly inside was a blue satin jewelry bag. After some fumbling, I managed to get the drawstring untied. At last, I was able to examine the watch, which had been beautifully refurbished.

"Oh my goodness, Mr. Perkins!" I exclaimed, happily. "It looks like new. How in the world did you do this? I mean, it's better than I ever expected! Where did you get the replacement parts? When I brought this in, you said they were nearly impossible to find."

"They are, but I promised I wouldn't give up until I found just what I needed. And Jethro Perkins always keeps his promises, even if his customers don't give him much time to get the job done."

"Sorry about that," I said, blushing slightly. "This pocket watch means so much to me. It belonged to my grandfather, and for as long as I can remember, he carried it with him. I guess that's why it's so special; it reminds me of all the good times we've shared together. Years ago, it played a little tune."

"It does again. Try it and see."

Carefully, I opened the watch to hear the familiar little Swiss melody ring through the shop. As I listened, tears welled up in my eyes. "I haven't heard this play for such a long time. The watch got damaged when I was in high school, and my grandfather never found a jeweler who could fix it. When I got engaged, I asked him if he still had the watch. He did, of course, and said I could give it to my fiancé as a wedding present if I wanted, only I'd need to find someone to repair it. I went to three other jewelers; they all told me it couldn't be fixed. You were my last hope when I brought it here. Thanks for working a miracle for me!"

"My pleasure, Julia. Check the engraving on the back. Did I get it right?"

Turning the watch over, I read the inscription. "It's perfect, Mr. Perkins. I can't wait to give it to David after our rehearsal dinner. How much do I owe you?"

With a sparkle in his eye, he pushed the bill across the counter. When I saw the price, I was sure he had made a mistake.

"Um…is this amount right?"

"Well, let's just say the bride got a discount."

"That's very generous of you," I expressed, writing out my check. "I don't know how to thank you."

"If you and your fella are happy together, that'll be thanks enough. Too many young people today want to get married but don't know how to *stay* married."

"Sad to say, you're right, Mr. Perkins. But I've been waiting so long for the right man, I don't intend to let him get away."

"Good for you. Keep thinkin' that way, and give the groom my best wishes when he opens his gift. Be sure to tell him where to bring the watch if he ever needs to get it repaired."

"I will. Thanks again," I replied before walking out the door.

When I returned to my car, a barking contest was going on between Sandy and a miniature poodle in the next vehicle. "Okay, girl, I'm back," I announced, easing behind the wheel. "That's enough barking." Turning around, I reached over and scratched a favorite spot behind the dog's ear. "Let's not pick up bad habits from others," I said with a smile.

Sandy settled down now that I was back in the car, but the poodle next door was continuing to send loud, threatening messages our way, frantically trying to squeeze its head through a cracked window. Even though the ongoing yelping was annoying, I couldn't resist taking a minute to look at the watch again. Removing it from the box, I pulled it out of the satin cover and re-read the inscription. With a contented sigh, I put it away again and acknowledged the *real* miracle worker: *Thank You, Lord. This watch being restored is an answer to prayer. You are good to me in so many ways, and I love and appreciate You so much.*

By now, Sandy couldn't resist growling under her breath at her noisy neighbor. Pacing back and forth on the seat, the large retriever tried to keep from barking again. Reaching back once more, I affectionately patted her. "Good girl, Sandy. It's not always easy to act like a lady, is it?"

As I turned to back out of the parking space, Sandy gave me an unexpected wet kiss on the cheek. Wiping my face, I ordered, "Down girl. I need to see to pull out. Just one more stop for gas, and we'll be seeing your master again this afternoon. Can't wait, can you?" Sandy was now lying on the seat, looking up at me with her big brown eyes, wagging her tail as though she understood every word.

Within minutes, my car was parked at the only unoccupied pump at the filling station. My family had been stopping at this same place for gas for almost fifty years, ever since my grandparents had bought land directly across from Crystal River and built their dream cottage.

For the past several days, I'd been staying at the cottage to spend some time alone with God before getting married. The Gordons, married friends of our family, were already up at our cottage doing repairs, so my parents let me go. They figured my solo getaway in such a secluded area would be safe with the Gordons there, too.

I had wanted this time away to re-read the journals I'd written to God while waiting to meet David—to reflect on all that had happened over the past few years and prepare my heart for our wedding on Saturday. My moment was finally here, and in a matter of days, my life would change forever. As I stood at the pump, I smiled at the thought of seeing David again in a few hours.

Suddenly, a loud click brought my attention back to the task at hand; my tank was full. Replacing the cap, I drove up to the convenience store to get some snacks and bottled water for the ride home. Once again, I had to leave Sandy in the car.

Walking toward the store, I looked overhead to see a threatening cloud cover rolling in from the west. Since I was heading east, I hoped to drive out of any storm that might be brewing.

After using the restroom, I quickly picked out the snacks I wanted and greeted the young cashier at the checkout counter. Chad worked there during his summer breaks, and I'd talked with him many times over the years.

"You going back to the cottage now?" he inquired.

"No, I decided to head back to Weston a day early."

"Well, be careful," he warned. "Two county officers just left; they said there's a severe storm alert out for this area until noon."

Turning to look out the store window, I could see it was getting darker by the minute. "Think I can get ahead of the bad weather?"

"Well, there's a shortcut off the main highway I use when I'm going east. It'll save you twenty minutes or more, and it might get you out of here before the storm hits."

"I think I'll try it. The sooner I get back, the better."

Chad reached for a scrap of paper. "I'll write down the directions so you won't miss the turnoff. Woodland Road is the first right after you pass Junction 12 on County Road J," he recited as he jotted down the information. "Eventually, it runs into the main highway that takes you to Weston."

Taking the slip of paper from him, I tucked it into the back pocket of my jeans. Then I gathered up my purchases and thanked Chad for his help. "Have a great semester at school this fall," I added, heading for the door.

"Sure thing. Drive safely."

"Of course—I have a big date on Saturday, you know!"

Before getting on the road, I poured some water into a paper cup and gave Sandy a drink. "We're off, girl. Looks like we'll be trying to outrun some heavy rain."

Soon the two of us were cruising along County Road J. My favorite song was playing, and Sandy was lying contentedly in the back, her eyes closed. Twenty minutes later, the sign for Junction 12 appeared. I pulled out the directions from my pocket and glanced at them. Rain was starting to come down, so I switched on the wipers.

It wasn't long before we came to the turnoff. Seeing a small **WOODLAND ROAD** sign, I slowed down a little and made a right. I was glad I'd seen the sign in time to make my turn.

Several miles down the road, the moderate rain turned into a torrential downpour. Sharp bolts of lightning illuminated the darkened sky, and a loud clap of thunder startled Sandy out of her peaceful nap. The wind was picking up, too. The trees lining either side of the road were bending before my eyes, and I was no longer enjoying the drive. It was getting hard to see more than three feet ahead of me. The wipers were going full speed, but they could barely keep up with the amount of water pouring over the windshield.

Suddenly, I was gripped with fear. I'd never been in the middle of such a severe storm before, especially when driving. "Help me, Jesus!" I cried out.

There was no place to pull over, and I didn't dare stop, not knowing if someone might be coming up behind me. So I reduced my speed, fighting to see where I was going, trying to keep my car on the road.

Soon, visibility was all but gone. Unknowingly, I steered into a patch of road where the rain had created a mudslide. Without warning, my tires hydroplaned, sending my car sliding out of control toward a nearby ravine. I screamed as I felt the car slip over the edge, falling, falling, falling until it violently lurched and stopped.

Struggling to catch my breath, I resisted the impulse to panic. Whatever had just happened, I was still in one piece. Sandy seemed okay as well. Even so, my heart was racing, and my body was shaking all over. I knew I had to pull myself together and try to assess the situation.

My car had landed in the ravine with the driver's side tilted downward slightly, the passenger side tilted upward. I was hoping the car hadn't fallen too far down; maybe it had just felt like it when we'd gone over the side. The impact had killed the motor, so I turned off the ignition switch to save the battery.

The storm was still raging wildly outside; I'd have to wait for it to stop before trying to get out of the car. I was terrified at the thought of climbing out of the window while keeping the car steady.

Realizing I could at least call for help, I unbuckled my seat belt to get my cell phone out of my purse. But where was my purse? It wasn't anywhere in sight. Finding it wasn't going to be easy, either, due to the way the car was positioned. Without knowing how deep the ravine was or how much water might be in it, I was afraid that moving around in the car might cause it to slide even further downward.

As I contemplated my next move, another sharp flash of light appeared, followed by a resounding clap of thunder and a loud cracking sound. Suddenly, a large tree hit by that last bolt of lightening came crashing down on top of the car. I screamed and threw my arms up over my head for protection as the roof, dashboard, and entire passenger side were crushed inward.

Gasping, I realized I was now wedged in the driver's seat, pinned under the steering wheel, unable to move. I frantically tried to move the steering wheel up by pulling on the side lever, but it wouldn't budge. Horrified, I just sat there in disbelief, trying not to hyperventilate.

After the initial wave of panic passed, I took a couple of slow breaths to get control of myself again. My first concern was for Sandy in the back seat. I'd heard a yelp when the tree hit but no movement since. Just as I started to call out to her, Sandy's head appeared through the open space between the front seats, and she began licking my outstretched hand. From all appearances, the retriever was all right. Most likely, she'd simply been temporarily stunned.

"I'm okay, too, girl," I assured her, gently stroking her head, grateful we were both still alive.

For the next few minutes, I said nothing, did nothing. I was too overwhelmed by what had just happened to think straight; I was in a daze.

Eventually, the storm outside subsided. The worst seemed to be over, weather-wise. My front windshield was shattered, and the windows on the passenger side of the car were smashed in. Glass was strewn throughout the interior of the vehicle. Some rain was getting in, but the fallen tree was keeping most of it out, acting as an umbrella. Since I couldn't see anything but branches, I had no idea if the impact from the tree had pushed the car any further down into the ravine.

Now that the storm had ended, I expected traffic to resume on Woodland Road. Yet I hadn't heard one car so far. Knowing nobody would find me unless I started making some noise, I pushed against the horn. Nothing. Startled, I pushed it again and again and again! Still nothing. Panicking, I stretched to turn on the radio. It wouldn't work either.

Terror gripped me as I realized I was totally helpless. That's when I lost it—now I was screaming at the top of my lungs between sobs for somebody, anybody to help me! I yelled out over and over, but there was nobody around to hear me.

All my crying and yelling had upset Sandy. She kept nudging my arm as if to ask what was wrong. Pausing to reassure her had a calming effect on me as well.

Emotionally exhausted, all I wanted to do was rest my head for a few minutes. I tried to recline my seat, but it wouldn't move. Untying the sweater I had wrapped around my waist, I shook out the glass particles. Then I tucked it between my head and the side window and closed my eyes.

When I opened my eyes again, all was quiet. Warm rays from the sun were filtering through the branches covering the car. I must have fallen asleep—no doubt in shock from the trauma of the accident. But how long had I been out? I didn't know. What was I going to do now? My purse was somewhere in the car, but where? It obviously went flying when we hit the ravine; it could be lying anywhere, possibly under my seat. Wherever it had gone, it was beyond my reach.

A feeling of desperation swept over me once again. All hope of being rescued began to fade as I reviewed my situation. I was returning home a day earlier than my parents and fiancé expected. I wouldn't even be missed until tomorrow around this time. Furthermore, my family would never think to look for me on Woodland Road. We didn't use this route; we always stuck to the main highway.

To make matters worse, could passing vehicles even see my car in the ravine with a huge tree covering it? And how could I get their attention with my radio and horn no longer working?

As I saw it, my only hope was Sandy. Pinned underneath this steering wheel, I couldn't go for help, but I could send her.

Unfortunately, that proved harder than I had anticipated. I ordered Sandy to go and get help several times, but the retriever was reluctant to leave my side. She would start out an open window only to turn around again and come back.

Then I remembered a game David and I used to play with Sandy in the park. I would cover the dog's eyes while David hid. Once he was out of sight, I'd release Sandy and shout, "Go find David, girl!" The retriever always found him, no matter how skillfully he tried to conceal himself.

I decided to try playing the game with Sandy. Covering her eyes for a few moments, I cried, "Go find David, girl!" This time Sandy squeezed her whole body through the window frame and disappeared into the branches of the tree. I waited and listened for a while for her to return. She didn't. She was out there somewhere, looking for her master.

Quickly, I sent up a prayer: *Father, Sandy's in Your hands now. In Jesus' name, help her to find someone— or for someone to find her. Then lead them back to me somehow.*

Done praying, I leaned my head over and rested again. There was nothing more to do but trust God and wait.

No Answer

A rustling sound in the tree overhead startled me. I froze in my seat, worried what animal might be approaching. Scanning the exposed window openings of the car, my eyes located the intruder. A friendly squirrel had dropped through the foliage and was now perched on the window frame.

Relieved, I smiled and watched my visitor munch away on an acorn for the next minute or so. When I squirmed in my seat to get more comfortable, the squirrel quickly scurried away. I was sorry to see it go. It felt good to have a living thing nearby. I knew I'd done the right thing by sending Sandy for help, but I felt so alone with her gone.

Gazing about the interior of the vehicle, I couldn't believe this was happening to me. Instead of a place of protection, my car felt more like a tomb as terror-filled thoughts flooded my mind: *You're trapped—Sandy's lost in the woods—Your wedding is ruined—You will never get out of here—They won't find you alive—You'll never see David or your family again…*

"No! That's not true!" I choked out, as tears coursed down my cheeks. Sobbing for a while, I finally got a grip on myself and forced a few deep breaths. Wiping my face with my hands, I cried out to the only One who could hear me. I started by reciting some verses I remembered from the New Living Translation of Psalm 91:

> "If you make the LORD your refuge, if you make the Most High your shelter, no evil will conquer you; no plague will come near your home. For he will order his angels to protect your wherever you go.

> "The LORD says, 'I will rescue those who love me. I will protect those who trust in my name. When they call on me, I will answer; I will be with them in trouble. I will rescue and honor them. I will reward them with a long life and give them my salvation.'"

Father, I will not give in to fearful thoughts meant to make me doubt You. I know You love me. You are here for me, and You have a way to get me out of this car! I refuse to accept that this will end badly for me. I have made You my refuge and my first love. I belong to You, Father! And the psalm I just quoted promises You will be with me in this trouble, that You will rescue me and show me Your salvation. It even says You will give me a long life. That's what I want, God: a long life, fulfilling the call You have for me. Like Romans 8:28 promises, You will work this accident for my good somehow.

*Please send help to me as quickly as possible, Father. I don't want to be stuck here long. I trust that Sandy is **not** lost, that You're giving her divine direction, getting her to someone who can help me. I don't have to know how You're going to do it or when; I just have confidence that You **will** get me out of here and back home safely. And my wedding is not ruined! I will walk away from this car and still be able to walk down the aisle to David on Saturday! God, Your promises aren't just words to me. I've seen them save me in the past, like when I was eighteen and trapped in that hotel room. I believe in the guardian angels You talk about in Psalm 91; please send them to help me now.*

David and I have waited so long for each other, Lord. I know You haven't brought us this far to separate us now; please don't let anything stop Your plan for us! As You know, we went through a lot to finally get engaged and have our wedding this weekend. But it's been worth it all, and I don't want to miss any of what comes next! I trust You to see me through this safely.

*I'm scared, Lord. But I give all my fear to You. According to 2 Timothy 1:7, You haven't given me "a spirit of fear, but of power and of love and of a sound mind." Fear, leave me **now**, and Father, please help me to feel Your presence as a reminder that You're with me.*

Even though my parents aren't expecting me home until tomorrow, please speak to my mom's heart—let her sense that something's wrong. I can't get to my cell phone to call her, but she can call me. If I don't answer, she'll keep trying; she won't rest until she tracks me down.

Thank You, Father, for hearing my prayer. Thank You for always being with me, for always taking care of me. I believe You're taking care of me right now, and I will not listen to any more crazy thoughts! I love You, Lord. All this I pray in Jesus' name.

As I finished my prayer, a peace settled over me that everything was going to be okay. For the first time since the accident, I was hungry. The water and snacks I'd picked up at the convenience store were fortunately within reach. The bottles had fallen off the seat and onto the floor when the car first hit the ravine, but they had rolled underneath my legs and were lying beside the door. Stretching, I was able to retrieve them both.

The snacks were in the console between the front seats. Opening the lid, I inventoried my supplies: two bottles of water, a bag of trail mix, and a protein bar.

These items would have to be rationed since I didn't know when help would arrive. It was the middle of August, very hot and humid, and although the tree covering the car was shielding me from the sun, I was still sweating a lot and was quite uncomfortable. I would have to drink to keep from getting dehydrated, but just a few sips at a time, spaced out over intervals. I didn't want to think about what I'd have to do if I needed to go to the bathroom!

I opened the protein bar first and broke off a fourth of it, nibbling it slowly, chewing and savoring every bite until it was gone. Next, I took a sip of water, holding it in my mouth for a while. Finally, I swallowed it and waited. Then I took a second sip and replaced the cap on the bottle.

Hysterical crying takes a lot out of a person; I was ready to rest again. How we take the little things in life for granted. At that moment, I would've given anything to be able to lie flat and stretch out my legs! Nevertheless, I shifted into a better position and was able to doze for a little while.

My sleep was interrupted by the muffled sound of musical notes playing. Startled, I put out my hand to shut off my clock radio, but I couldn't quite reach it...

Opening my eyes, I painfully remembered that I was trapped in my car, not sleeping in my room! The sound I heard was coming from somewhere behind me. Fully awake now, I recognized the melody: *Here Comes the Bride*. I had programmed it as my ringtone weeks ago. Someone was calling my cell phone.

That's my mom! I thought, excited. *Or maybe David. No, it can't be David. We agreed not to talk until I got home from the cottage tomorrow. It must be Mom calling.*

The music stopped abruptly; all was silent again. Smiling, I envisioned my mom getting no answer and leaving a message for me to call her. *Thank You, Father, for answering my prayer!*

I was sure my mom was already sensing that something was wrong, and I knew her—when I didn't return her call in a reasonable amount of time, the search would be underway. My part was to hang on until my family found me.

Lord, while I'm waiting, please give me something constructive to do. I don't know how soon it will be before my family puts all the pieces together and finds me. Keep my mind focused to protect it from thinking the worst. The longer I have to wait, the easier it will be to lose hope.

But what was there to do? My journals and Bible were inside my suitcase in the trunk. Besides, even though it was daytime, there wasn't enough light inside the car for reading. The only thing left was my mind. I needed something to think about to keep myself occupied.

Since I was fighting such fear about my wedding being ruined, I decided to dream about how I wanted this weekend to still go. I pictured getting rescued and seeing David again. I mentally rehearsed calling all my bridesmaids to tell them I was fine. I thought about what I was going to wear to my rehearsal dinner Friday night, pushing down thoughts of having any major injuries that would mess anything up. I visualized getting ready, fixing my hair and makeup, doing everything with the excitement of knowing that the next day I'd be marrying David.

Sighing, I returned to the present to have another snack. This time, I opened the trail mix bag and poured out a generous handful. Instead of putting it in my mouth all at once, I began eating one morsel at a time, chewing it thoroughly.

Soon I heard a scrambling sound to the side of me. *Plop*—another squirrel fell through the tree. He seemed a bit braver than the first one, so I took a few of my nuts and threw them on the floor behind the passenger seat. The little squirrel scampered to where they had landed. I enjoyed watching him through the opening between the front seats as he ate them up. When I tossed a few more his way, he sat up, looking at me as if to say *thanks*.

"Taste good?" I asked, getting only a slight nose twitch in return. I wanted to give him more, but I knew this was all the food I had. Thirsty, I reached for a bottle of water and took a sip. When I looked back, the squirrel was gone.

"Bye!" I called out behind him. It felt good to talk aloud to someone, even if it was only a squirrel!

Taking a few more sips of my water, I placed the cap back on the bottle. The muscles in my back were getting strained from the car's angle. Trying to get some relief, I squirmed in my seat, turning my upper body until I felt more comfortable. Now I was ready to keep dreaming.

I pictured waking up Saturday morning and heading to the salon with my bridesmaids. After lots of well wishing, compliments, and laughter with my best friends, my hair would turn out just how I'd always wanted it to look on my wedding day. Feeling like a pampered princess, I'd head to the church to put on the beautiful gown I'd been dreaming of wearing for months. No worries. No thoughts of this ridiculous car accident. Everything just as I had planned all along...

I took a break from my musings and ate the rest of my protein bar, too hungry to save any of it for later. I wondered if my family had started to look for me yet. Hopefully, I would be found before dark. The thought of spending the night alone in my car was a little frightening. Then I reminded myself that I wasn't alone. The Lord was here with me.

No Fairy Tale

I continued to keep my mind occupied on good things for several hours. Or did it just seem that long, pinned under my steering wheel? I was ready for a break, to stop trying so hard to be optimistic about what would happen in the days and weeks to come.

Reaching for a water bottle, I took a few sips. Leaning my head back, I listened to the sounds filtering in from overhead—birds chirping, leaves flapping in the wind, forest creatures and insects calling out to each other. If I hadn't been trapped in my car under a tree, I would have enjoyed this tranquil little symphony. But the longer I waited for help, the more I had to cast down negative thoughts that no one was coming for me.

All I wanted to do now was forget where I was and think about David. My David. Our courtship had clearly been no fairy tale, certainly more complicated than the typical storybook romance. But it was our story, and I loved it.

Thinking back, the day I met David started out like most days since coming home from Tyler University. Nothing indicated I was about to meet my man. In fact, I'd been experiencing more than the usual amount of frustration about not having a boyfriend—similar to what I'd gone through my second semester at Tyler, before dating Jay. How happy I was to have that bad relationship behind me!

But now I was having to deal with Paul, my friend from church. He was in love with me, convinced we were perfect for each other. He was certain that I loved him, too, and accused me of denying my feelings for him because of the way Jay had abused me in the past.

Most of the time, I was sure Paul was wrong. I believed God had told me to stop seeing him, so I had. But somewhere in the back of my mind, there was the nagging fear that perhaps he *was* right. Maybe what happened with Jay *had* caused me to seal up my heart. I was attracted to Paul and enjoyed being with him, but he wanted to go back to the West Coast to start an accounting firm. I wanted to stay in Weston. To him that was a minor problem—to me it was the deciding factor.

It was getting harder for me to resist him because I was tired of waiting to meet my Mr. Right. When my friends Flip and Melody announced their engagement, it almost pushed me over the edge. I journaled to God about my frustrations, and when I was finished, a wonderful change had taken place in my heart: my obsessive desire for a boyfriend had been dealt with once again. I made the choice to be truly content as a single for this season, trusting my Heavenly Father for the *timing* of my love story. I had no idea it would begin that very night as I visited a recovering friend in the hospital.

Meeting David in the cafeteria took me completely by surprise. Why would this handsome doctor ask to sit at my table? The room wasn't crowded. I didn't know what else to do, so I nodded that it was okay. For the next few moments, I felt like I was back at Tyler University, meeting Jay for the first time at The Coffee Cup. Everything was so similar.

It was easy for me to talk to David from the very beginning. He had a great sense of humor and was an excellent listener. I couldn't help but notice how good looking and nice he was, but I reminded myself not to read into his attention. He was just someone new to the area trying to make friends.

From our conversation, I found out he was a Christian and had been invited to our church. Naturally, I offered to introduce him around when he came to the service the next morning. Finishing our conversation in the cafeteria, we left the hospital together, saying our goodbyes in the parking lot.

When we separated to find our cars, we didn't think we'd be seeing each other again quite so soon. I sure didn't expect to run into a former professor in the parking lot. I was startled to open my car door, turn, and find creepy Don McNulty standing directly behind me. Before I knew it, he was in my face, threatening me, trying to kiss me. I could tell he'd been drinking, and I was terrified he was going to push me into my car and rape me. Fortunately, David heard my screams and came to my rescue. How thankful I was that he was still around! Who knows what would have happened had he not been there that night?

I was rattled after McNulty's attack, but there was something about David that put me at ease—maybe his voice, how he took charge, the way he looked at me, his smile. Whatever it was, I felt safe with him, confident he could be trusted. My favorite part of David bringing me home that night was when he had to carry me inside to my room because I was in shock and too weak to walk.

Even though I was exhausted from my ordeal, I had to pray before falling asleep. My meeting with David earlier that evening baffled me. I couldn't understand why it so mirrored the first time I had met Jay. I asked God to explain the why of it someday, knowing there had to be some significance. It wasn't until David and I were dating that I got my answer. The similarities were meant to show me how a counterfeit like Jay can resemble the real thing. My Heavenly Father wanted me to know for sure that *David* was my real love—the man God had handpicked for me.

But I had no idea when I fell asleep that night that my future husband was downstairs talking with my parents! At that stage in our relationship, I was happy to simply be his friend. I liked David, respected him as a doctor, and felt I could help him plug into our church and start his life in Weston. Expecting more from a man like him was more than my heart was ready to risk.

As he promised the night before, David attended the Sunday morning service at our church the next day. Happy to see him again, I invited him to sit with my family. Paul came in soon after the music began and found a seat in a pew off to the right of us. He smiled at me, as usual, then turned his eyes to the front and began worshipping.

Once the congregation was dismissed, I began introducing David to the people around us. My best friend and her fiancé were sitting behind us, so David met Cassie and Brian first. While the four of us were talking, Paul walked up and asked, "Who's this, Julia?"

It was obvious from Paul's tone and expression that he'd already decided not to like whoever this was. David did his best to be cordial, shaking Paul's hand, asking what he did, where he worked, the usual small talk. But even David could see he was getting the cold shoulder for some reason. I knew the reason: Paul was jealous.

Although I had enjoyed my friendship with Paul in the past, I was getting tired of his attitude. Since he was taking his CPA exam soon, I'd been praying that he would pass the first time and return to the West Coast. I wanted closure on our relationship, but that didn't seem possible as long as he was still in town and we were going to the same church. Paul had only come to Weston U. to get his degree. Now his plan to return to his hometown and start his own business included taking *me* with him. He stubbornly refused to accept the fact that I did not want to marry him and move away.

His behavior toward my guest that Sunday was so embarrassing. I was ashamed of him for acting the way he did, and concerned that David might be offended by his rudeness. Fortunately, it didn't seem to bother David. Apparently, he knew how to deal with difficult people.

My dad invited David to join our family for lunch after church, but he had another commitment. My parents and I ate at a restaurant downtown and then stopped by the hospital to pick up my car that was still there from my run-in with McNulty. Even though it was daylight, being in the same parking lot where it had happened sent chills shooting up my spine. I was glad when I was in my car and away from there.

Driving home alone, feelings of hatred toward Don McNulty flooded my heart as I remembered how he had forced himself on me the night before. Suddenly, my thoughts were interrupted with, "Julia, I love Don."

Startled, I looked around, as though someone inside the car had said those words. Then I realized it was the Lord speaking to my spirit.

How can You love him, Father? He's a terrible, terrible man! Ugh! He makes me sick!

"I don't like the things he does, but I do understand why he does them. He's been deeply hurt, Julia. Pray for him."

Pray for him? The thought seemed absurd to me. Pray for him how? I was the victim, not him. Or *was* I the only one? Suddenly, I remembered something my pastor had pointed out in a recent message on forgiveness. He had said that *hurting people hurt others*. Was this what God was trying to tell me, that McNulty had hurt me because he was hurting within himself?

I knew he drank and had a problem with sexually harassing students, but I'd never stopped to think there must be a reason. I wasn't being asked to figure that out; I didn't need to know those details. God just wanted me to forgive McNulty for what he had done to me and then pray for someone to come along who could help him receive Christ and work through his painful past.

By the time I got home, I was willing to do that. Not because I felt like it. Truthfully, I didn't. What had happened was still fresh and painful, but because I loved and trusted my Heavenly Father, I went to my room and knelt by my bed, speaking words that had nothing to do with my feelings and everything to do with my will.

Afterwards, I felt much lighter, not because the hurt was completely gone from the night before, but from the satisfaction and peace that comes from doing the right thing, from letting go of what isn't yours to bear. I knew that in time, I'd be able to have more compassion for McNulty, maybe even pray for him with God's kind of love. But for now, the choice to forgive and pray a blessing over him was enough.

Even so, McNulty still had to be confronted and dealt with to prevent him from doing the same thing to other women.

Since my father had done a lot of legal work for the university over the years, he knew the president and called early Monday morning to tell him what had happened Saturday night. My dad also filled him in on the times McNulty had harassed me in the past. It took a few days to coordinate everyone's schedule, but a meeting was set up for Friday afternoon to address the issue.

I saw David briefly on Wednesday as he looked in on patients at Sunny Acres Rehabilitation Center, where I worked in the physical therapy wing. He could tell I was uptight about seeing McNulty again.

"Don't worry, Julia. Everything's going to be all right. Your dad and I will both be there with you. Hopefully, you won't have to say a word if you don't want to."

"Thanks, Dr. Stanton," I replied, careful not to call him by his first name at work. "I'll see you on Friday."

When my dad and I got to the university president's office that day, David was already there, waiting. Professor McNulty arrived last. Once we were all seated, President Rogers presented my complaint to McNulty and asked him to respond.

I was shocked when he tried to blame me for the incident, saying I was nothing but a big flirt and had been chasing after him for a long time. He admitted he'd had a couple of drinks before seeing me in the parking lot that night, but he insisted I'd been the one to call him over to my car.

"She was pretty much begging me to kiss her. When I wouldn't, she started screaming her head off." Gesturing toward David, he added, "That's when this guy jumped me from behind and threw me against her car. They were both acting crazy, so I got out of there as fast as I could."

I was so upset by what he said, I couldn't speak. Tears began sliding down my cheeks. When David saw how those accusations hurt me, he couldn't restrain himself. Jumping up, he faced the professor seated to his right.

"You're a liar, McNulty! And not even a good one! Do you expect anyone to believe that Julia was trying to seduce you? No way! By the time I got to where she was screaming, you already had her pinned against her car. I saw you grabbing her hair with one hand and twisting her wrist with the other. *You* were the one forcing a kiss. She was struggling to get away from you when I pulled you off her." Turning to the president, David said, "If you care to examine Julia's wrist, you'll see that it's still bruised."

President Rogers quickly spoke to settle David down. "Please take your seat, Dr. Stanton. Be assured, I don't believe Professor McNulty's story for a minute." Speaking to the accused, he said, "You're forgetting something, Don. I've known Julia and her family for a long time. She may be friendly, but she's not a flirt. And neither was Emily Warden or Kayla Drayton. I still have their written complaints accusing you of sexual harassment. Of course, you denied those charges, and I only had their word against yours—no proof or eyewitnesses to back up their claims. But Julia's case against you is undeniable, thanks to Dr. Stanton.

"You've abused your position as a professor here at Weston University, Don. Who knows how many of our female students have been sexually harassed by you? My choice is clear. Effective immediately, you're finished on this campus. Leave your keys here on my desk. I'll have someone pack up your things from your office and bring them to you in the parking lot. In fact, security is waiting to escort you there when we're done with this meeting.

"I have Julia's written complaint as well as a copy of the police report; I'm adding them to your file. Obviously, I will not be giving you a recommendation to teach anywhere else. You are not allowed on university property after today. I'll get a restraining order if I have to, but that will take this public. I'm sure you'd rather avoid that."

The professor shot me a threatening look before starting to protest, but the president cut him off. "There's no need for discussion, Don. My decision is final." In closing, he looked around the room. "Does anyone else have anything to say before this meeting ends?"

My dad stood and turned to McNulty. "I don't want you coming anywhere near my daughter. If you see her walking down the street, cross over to the other side. If you see her car somewhere, start driving in the other direction. If you speak to her, call her, harass or threaten her in any way, I will use all my legal influence in this community to make your life miserable. You *will* go to jail. Do you understand me?"

"Is that a threat?" McNulty snapped back, beet red.

"Call it whatever you want. I'm not blind; I saw the hateful way you looked at my daughter just now. I'm simply making sure you know what to expect from me if you step out of line with her again. If you're smart, you'll get professional help, Don; you're a sick man."

McNulty didn't answer my dad. He simply got up, threw his keys on the president's desk, and stormed out of the room, a security officer close behind.

As we left that day, I thanked David for coming to my defense. He'd been right; I hadn't had to say anything during the meeting. He and my dad had ended up doing all the talking, and I was relieved. I was ready to forgive McNulty *again*, let him face the consequences for his wrongdoing, and put the whole incident behind me.

Gradually, I was learning to forgive the way God wants us to. Refusing to forgive only hurts you anyway; forgiveness helps set you free from what happened. This turned out to be a timely lesson since I'd have more forgiving to do soon.

Sending Daisies

David was in church again on Sunday. After service, I introduced him to our youth group leader. When Pastor Kevin heard that David had experience with teens at his last church, he told him a little about our youth program. "One of my leaders is moving, so I need to replace him," he added. "There are ten boys in his group. I think you'd like them. Would you be interested in the position?"

"Sure," David replied without hesitation.

"Great," Pastor Kevin responded, pulling a servant application from his Bible. "Fill this out and turn it in to the church office. I'll get back to you sometime next week after checking your references."

As Pastor Kevin walked away, I smiled at David, happy he was getting involved in church right away. At the same time, I realized that both Paul and I were already leaders in the youth program; if David accepted the position, we would all be attending leadership meetings together. Things could get very interesting.

Brian and Cassie were still talking outside the church when David and I came out. Cassie motioned us over. "We're going to Benny's to grab some lunch. You two want to come with us?"

David looked at me. "Okay with you?"

"Sure, do you know how to get there?"

"Yeah, I know where it is."

"Okay," Brian said. "Cass and I will meet you there."

David arrived at Benny's a little ahead of me and waited up front. When I came in, the hostess led us toward the back of the restaurant to the last available booth. Knowing Brian and Cassie would want to sit next to each other, David suggested that he and I sit together. Always the gentleman, he let me slide in first. It felt a little awkward sitting there side by side with him with nobody across from us. *What message is this sending?* I wondered.

Benny's had been our singles' hangout for years. As I looked around the restaurant, I noticed several people from our church watching David and me to see what was going on between us. One annoying part of being single is that the minute you're seen alone with a guy in public or even just talking with him a lot, people begin to wonder if romance is involved. Then you have to put up with all the nosy comments and questions that follow.

That was the last thing I wanted to happen. I was thankful to David for all he had done for me since we'd met, and I was looking forward to getting to know him better. Because he was already a doctor and more mature than some of my friends, I was afraid that any matchmaking foolishness would bother him.

We sat in the booth waiting for Brian and Cassie for over twenty minutes. I couldn't imagine what was taking them so long. David asked me if I wanted to order an appetizer while we waited, but I didn't want to spoil my meal. Just as I was pulling out my phone to text Cassie, David saw them walk through the front door.

"Here they are, Julia."

I looked up to see they weren't the only ones arriving. Flip and Melody had come in at the same time, with Paul. I tried not to show my concern and was relieved when the three of them took a table that had opened up near the front.

Meanwhile, Brian saw David wave from the back of the restaurant, and he and Cassie quickly made their way to our booth. "Sorry we're late, Dr. Stanton," he apologized. "There was an accident a few blocks away; we got held up in traffic."

David stood while Cassie was getting into the booth and shook Brian's hand. "You guys can call me David, you know," he said once everyone was seated.

"Oh, I like that much better," Cassie admitted, leaning forward as if she were about to add something important. "It's hard to be friends with someone you have to keep calling doctor something or other."

David laughed with the rest of us. "Exactly my point."

"Anyone else hungry?" she continued. "I'm starved!"

Brian looked at me and winked. "Imagine that!"

Everyone was laughing except David. "Inside joke?" he asked.

"The joke's on me," Brian assured him. "I'm marrying a woman who can out-eat two men, and I get to support her appetite the rest of my life!"

Cassie playfully hit his arm in protest before asking, "Where's our waitress, anyway? I'm getting the special, whatever it is."

David smiled at Brian and shook his head. "We'd better get some food into your fiancée before she faints." Then he waved the server over, and we placed our orders.

For the next hour, I forgot all about being watched by anyone. I was having a wonderful time just being myself, talking and laughing over a meal with friends. I realized I wasn't feeling lonely for the first time in a long time. Something had changed, but I couldn't pinpoint when that empty feeling had disappeared.

At the time, I attributed not feeling lonely anymore to having a new friend. David and I had a lot of fun together, he was great to talk to, and he made me feel like what I said was valuable. That was all I needed to know for the moment. I wasn't going to hope for any more right now. This was enough.

My friends at the front table finished eating ahead of us and started back to say hello—all *three* of them. David already knew Paul. He'd just met Flip and Melody that morning before church.

"Nice to see you again, Dr. Stanton," Paul remarked flatly when they reached our booth.

David read his sarcasm. "I'm sure you'll be seeing a lot more of me, Paul."

The expression on Paul's face showed how much that irritated him. Trying to ease the tension, David turned to Flip. "Julia tells me you're the best mechanic in town."

"Yeah, we kinda do the same thing, you and me. You fix sick people; I fix sick cars."

"Then I've got a patient for you, Flip."

"You mean that sweet foreign job parked out front?"

"That's the one."

Flip grinned, obviously excited to work on it. "What's the problem?"

"I'm not sure. The motor's been running rough lately. It might just need a good tune-up. I'd like you to check it out."

"Sure thing. Drop it off in the mornin' at eight, and I'll take care of ya." Reaching into his pocket, he handed his business card to David.

"That's west of here, right?" David asked, scanning the card.

"Right. Get on the bypass and exit left onto Fifth. Wells Street is about six blocks down. An' I'm on the corner. Ya can't miss it."

"Thanks, I'll find it."

So far, no one had said much to Melody. David inserted Flip's card into his wallet and asked her, "Have you two set a wedding date?"

Melody smiled, glad to be included in the conversation. "Yes, a year from now, the second Saturday in April."

"Have you found your dress?" I broke in.

"No, I haven't been shopping yet. I know you're busy helping Cassie with her wedding, but I thought you might like to come with my mom and me when I go looking. I'm terrible at making big decisions like this; I'd love your opinion."

Paul shocked me by responding, "Julia will go with you. She'll probably need a dress herself soon."

David saw me blush. "Really?" he answered, raising his eyebrows and smiling at Paul. "Well, no doubt she'll be a beautiful bride whenever she chooses to get married."

Everyone could see from his expression that David's response made Paul mad. Refusing to look at him, I told Melody I'd be happy to help her pick out a dress. She thanked me and said she'd text me toward the end of the week. Flip could tell that Paul was fuming, so he stepped in, made some excuse to leave, and got his friend out of there.

After a few moments of awkward silence, Cassie suggested we all get going. We were finished eating, and people were waiting to be seated. While the men shook hands goodbye, Cassie looked my way and mouthed she'd call me later. Brian left cash on the table for their part of the bill, and he and Cassie were out the door.

As David and I walked to the register, he asked if he could pay for my meal. My past had been riddled with men who tried to push what *they* wanted on me. How refreshing to be with someone who cared about what I might want. The difference was a welcome change, and I graciously accepted his offer.

As David walked me to my car, I could sense he had something on his mind. He waited until I had unlocked my door to ask, "Julia, is there something between you and Paul I should know about? He acts like there is."

"Only in his mind."

"You're sure? Because as much as your friendship means to me, I don't want to cause any trouble between you."

"You're not causing any trouble, David. Paul's just being difficult. He's been going to our church for a few years, and we used to hang out a lot as friends. Eventually, he wanted more. I knew we wanted different things for our lives, so I stopped spending time with him. He's having a hard time accepting that I don't want to marry him."

"It doesn't look like he's trying very hard. Does he think he's scoring points with you by acting the way he does?"

"That's the problem, David. He doesn't get that there is no more score; the game's over. I'm sorry he's taking his disappointment out on you."

"Don't worry about it, Julia. I can handle him. I just wanted to make sure I understood the situation. I've got some time off this Wednesday. Want to play some racquetball?"

"My last rehab patient is at one o'clock, but I should be finished by two-thirty. I could meet you at the Y around three?"

"Okay, I'll call and reserve a court." David pulled out a business card and handed it to me. "Call my cell if your plans change. Otherwise, I'll see you on Wednesday at three."

As usual when you're looking forward to something, time drags along. I saw David in passing at work a few times on Monday and Tuesday, but we didn't get to say much more than hello. Either he was tied up with a resident, or I was busy in rehab. His visits to the Center were brief and not necessarily every day. Most of his time was taken up with office appointments and hospital rounds.

Before leaving for work on Wednesday, I packed a bag to take to the Y. Although I wouldn't admit to liking David as more than a friend, it took me a good ten minutes to pick out some shorts and a T-shirt to play in. My clothes would probably be wringing wet after our match, but I at least wanted to start out looking good!

My morning at the Center went well. The majority of the residents were in good spirits. When you're working with the elderly, you appreciate those days. They are sometimes few and far between. Even difficult Mr. Quinn was more chipper than usual. We breezed through his program, allowing me to finish my shift on time.

David was already at the Y when I arrived. "Nice outfit," he commented as I walked in wearing my Center uniform.

I held up my gym bag. "Give me five minutes to change."

"You women like to keep us men waiting, don't you?"

"But we're so worth it. Besides, it'll give you time to rest up before I run your legs off."

"Oh, the lady talks a little smack! We'll see..."

When I came out of the locker room, David pointed toward court two. "I haven't played for a while," he reminded me as we walked inside. "Don't be too rough on me today."

I laughed. "Can't promise..."

Once we were on the court, David offered to let me serve first. For the next hour, we both ran our legs off. David was a great player. I was keeping up with him by the score, but I could tell he wasn't playing all out against me. When we were finished, I made him fess up.

"All right, tell me the truth. You could've creamed me if you'd wanted to." Smiling, he handed me a clean towel and led me over to a bench where we could sit down, dry off, and catch our breath. "Be honest," I persisted.

"What would've been the point in that?" he asked, wiping the back of his neck. "Neither of us came here to prove anything; we're just here to have fun. And we did. At least I did."

"Me, too," I smiled.

"You're an excellent player, Julia. You have a great serve and keep good pace on the ball. I had to work hard to stay ahead of you. Who taught you to play so well?" he asked, taking a sip of his sports drink.

"My grandma."

David almost choked in the middle of a swallow. Half-laughing, he said, "Your grandmother taught you to play racquetball? The one I met at church? I don't believe it."

Now I was laughing. "Okay, it was my brother, John. We've always been close, and when I was in middle school, he started bringing me here to play. We used to come a lot. He was pretty nice while I was learning, but now he shows no mercy. I rarely beat him anymore."

"Does your brother live in Weston?"

"Actually, he's in South America, working as an engineer in Chile. He's been there almost four years. He'll be coming home again in August with his wife and little girl. I can't wait to see them."

"When he gets back, I'll ask him to play. Any other siblings?"

"No, only John. How about you?"

"Just one sister—Carrie. We were close, too. She was such a beautiful person, inside and out."

"Was?"

"She got cancer when she was in college; she died about five years ago."

"Oh, David. I'm so sorry. I can't imagine not having John anymore."

"I really miss her, Julia. Carrie's death was difficult for our whole family. My mother still isn't over it."

"She'll heal in time," I assured him.

"I hope so. That's what my dad and I keep praying for." As he said that, sadness filled his eyes. "It's a long story, Julia. Someday I'd like to tell you more, but I need to get back to the hospital to make some rounds. Ready to go?"

"Sure. Thanks for playing, David. I had a great time."

"We'll do it again soon," he promised.

Exiting the court, we said our goodbyes and separated to go to the locker rooms to shower and change. I was tired, sweaty, and very happy. There was something about David—something I couldn't put into words. All I knew was I couldn't wait to see him again.

When I left the Y, I went on campus to do some research at the library. How glad I would be when my last courses were completed and I finally had my master's degree! Working during the day with classes at night was a bigger challenge than I had anticipated. Fortunately, I finished what I needed to do at the library in about an hour and made it back home around suppertime.

As I walked into the kitchen, my mom and our maid, Kitty, were working at the stove, putting the finishing touches on dinner.

"Good timing, honey," my mom said over her shoulder. "We'll be eating soon. Something came for you a few minutes ago. I put it on the table in the foyer."

I wondered what it could be. Setting my purse on the counter, I headed for the foyer, where I spotted a long white box on the mahogany side table next to the staircase. As I got closer, I could read the name on the lid—Lyndall's Floral Shop.

"Oh, no," I moaned, knowing Paul was the accountant there. No doubt he'd sent these flowers to make amends for the way he had acted at Benny's. I was getting so tired of dealing with yet another thing with Paul!

Getting flowers is supposed to make a girl happy, but I didn't want to be obligated to thank Paul for sending them. He was sure to take what was merely a polite response the wrong way. Still, I had no choice. The flowers had already been delivered; I'd have to accept them.

Lifting the lid, I looked in the box. Nestled inside were a dozen of the most beautiful daisies I had ever seen. Curious to read Paul's apology, I pulled out the card. I was stunned at first but extremely happy. The flowers weren't from Paul after all; they were from David.

Julia,
I'm sending daisies to say thanks for being my friend.
David

"Thanks for being my friend," I recited. My mother heard me from the dining room where she was setting food out on the table. She stopped what she was doing, came into the foyer, and stood next to me.

"Look, Mom—aren't these beautiful?"

"Lovely," she agreed as I handed her the card. As she read it, my dad got up from his favorite chair in the living room and joined us.

"Very pretty," he remarked, looking into the box. "Who sent them?"

"David."

"Looks like Julia and David are in *the friendship stage*," my mom added with a twinkle in her eye.

"That's nice," my dad replied, heading back into the living room, oblivious to the point my mom was trying to make.

I, on the other hand, understood her perfectly.

A Cinderella Story

Because dinner was already on the table, I postponed putting my flowers in water until after we'd eaten. As soon as we finished, I helped clear the table and then ran upstairs to my room, looking for the crystal vase my grandmother had given me several years before.

My grandma called it my *suitor vase*—to be used for flowers I would receive from a boyfriend one day. It was meant to give me hope that someday such flowers *would* come, but at the time, my grandma's gift did little to cheer me up. Instead of displaying it somewhere, I stuck it on a shelf in my closet where I wouldn't have to be daily reminded that it was still empty! I was excited to finally bring the vase out of hiding and use it for the daisies David had sent me.

When I found it in my closet, the vase was *very* dusty from sitting so long. I had to wash it twice with hot sudsy water and use a soft-bristle brush to remove some stubborn residue from the crevices. When the vase was clean and dried, it sparkled brilliantly under the lights in the kitchen. It was so much more beautiful than I had remembered. I guess everything looks better when you're not feeling sorry for yourself.

I filled the vase with water and, after diagonally snipping the stems, transferred the daisies into it one by one. Adding the sprigs of greenery included in the box, I proudly stood back to examine my arrangement. It was lovely.

While my parents admired my handiwork, I cleaned up the mess on the counter. Then I took the vase and David's card up to my room where I placed them on my desk.

David probably sent daisies because they looked more like friendship than roses would have, yet what he didn't know was that daisies were my favorite. I couldn't stop smiling as I re-read David's card. Those words meant so much to me. I'd been without a close guy friend for so long; now I had one again.

Inside the window seat in my room, I kept an empty keepsake box. I walked over and pulled it out. I had bought this to eventually store mementos from my Mr. Right—things like ticket stubs, pictures, or any notes or letters he might send me one day.

I placed David's card inside the box, but instead of returning it to the window seat, I cleared off a space on my desk by the flowers and set it there. It was too much to hope that David could actually be my Mr. Right, but his card was special to me, and I wanted to keep it close.

My mom had said earlier that David and I were in *the friendship stage.* My dad didn't know what she was getting at, but I did. She was referring to a long talk we had in a restaurant years ago, when she explained relationships to me. She meant David and I were in the stage where a couple gets to know each other better—to see if they relate well, to decide if they want to move into a deeper level of commitment. I had never gotten past the friendship stage with Paul because he and I had different visions for our lives. That's why I had to end things between us before we were in too deep to turn back.

But what about David and me, Lord? What if we are headed for the same unhappy ending? What if our friendship ends in frustration for one of us like the situation with Paul? I didn't want to think about that happening.

Lord, please help me not to worry about things that may never happen. Help me to enjoy the good of today and trust You for my tomorrow. For now, I see no warning signs, no reason not to enjoy being friends with David. I trust You for whatever comes of this friendship. Neither David nor I know what lies down the road, but You do. Please give us the courage to simply walk it out and see. I have faith, Lord, that You will always be here to direct us, that either way— friends or more—neither one of us will get hurt.

Ready to get my mind on something else, I got online and sent an email to my brother and his wife.

I was counting the days until they would be home, aching to see them again. Jenny was like a real sister to me; I loved talking with her, which was often. The next time Jenny called, I planned to tell her about David.

I was looking forward to something else, too: seeing my elderly friend, Miss Lottie, again. She lived in the apartments next door to the Center and came in almost every day to visit the residents. We had become close during my years of working there.

Miss Lottie had left town abruptly to be with her sister who had suffered a stroke. I hadn't talked with her since meeting David at the hospital and was anxious to fill her in on all the details, including the McNulty incident. I didn't plan to tell her about my daisies, though, because I knew she liked to play Cupid.

I had just started going through my research notes from the library when I heard my mom call for me to come downstairs. When I reached the foyer, I saw Cassie standing in the living room, talking with my parents. She was visibly upset.

"What's wrong?" I asked, anxiously. "Is Brian all right?"

"He's fine, but our wedding isn't."

"What do you mean? You guys didn't have a fight, did you?"

"No, nothing like that. We just don't have anywhere to hold our reception now. There was a fire this morning at Keldon's. My mom heard about it on the radio and drove over to check out the damage.

It's pretty bad. Even if the owners rebuild the hall, it won't be ready by July. We've been on the phone all day trying to find another place, but everything around here is already booked. We don't know what to do," Cassie admitted, teary-eyed.

My dad smiled reassuringly at Cassie. "Don't give up yet, Cass. Let's sit down. We'll figure out something." Once we were all seated, he asked, "Where's Brian?"

"Still down at the office."

"Finishing up the Ebson case?"

"I'm not sure. He said he'd be working late."

"Sorry, Cassie. I'd tell him to come right over if that work didn't have to be finished for a court appearance tomorrow. You say your mom checked every banquet hall around, and they're all booked for your date?"

"All except one, Mr. Duncan. The country club had a cancellation for our Saturday, but they might as well be booked as far as we're concerned. Their prices are way beyond what we can pay."

My mom spoke up. "Cassie, if you *could* afford the country club, would it be large enough for all your guests? I think it can accommodate one hundred fifty, maybe two hundred if the terrace is set up. That's where my niece had her reception."

"That would be more than enough room, Mrs. Duncan, but Brian and I don't want to start off together in debt. We'd need a miracle to pay cash for it."

"Well, we serve a miracle-working God, don't we?" my mom reminded her. Turning toward my dad, she smiled. "Doesn't Calvin from the club owe you a favor?"

My dad was already pulling out his cell phone. "This might be the perfect time to take advantage of his offer. Let's see what I can do here." Scrolling through his contacts, he found the number and made the call.

"Calvin?...Phil Duncan here. Glad to find you home. How's the family?...That's good. I'll tell you why I called. I'm trying to help some young people close to our family get married. You know Brian Douglas from my office?...Yes, he *is* a great young man. Well, he's marrying Julia's best friend; she's like a daughter to me. Their wedding date is the fifteenth of July, and the hall they had booked burned down today... Yes, Keldon's. Every other banquet facility around is taken, with the exception of yours. Apparently, there was a recent cancellation at your club for that date.

"Cal, I really need your help on this one. The bride is sitting here in my living room about to cry her eyes out. Please book that date for me before someone else does...Well, then call the wedding coordinator tonight. She won't mind...Great! That's settled.

"Since we've got an emergency situation here, let's talk about how we can help these kids out with the cost. You told me when my firm won that big case for you, saving you *millions*, that if I ever needed anything, just ask...I know you meant it, Cal. Now I'm asking. What kind of a deal are we talking here? Uh huh...Too much...No, still too high..."

Listening as my dad worked out all the details with the owner, I saw why he was such a good attorney. By the end of the conversation, he had arranged for Brian and Cassie to have the dining room and terrace, hors d'oeuvres, dinner, beverages, sparkling grape juice for the toast, and even a beautiful cake. All they had to do was pay for gratuity and hire their own DJ.

Concluding the call, he said, "Okay, I'll have Cassie get in touch with your coordinator; they can go over the details tomorrow. By the way, I'll need to have what we agreed on tonight in writing. You know us lawyers. Have something typed up for me to look over, will you? Thanks again, Cal. You're a good man...I will. You have a great night, too."

When my dad hung up, he grinned at Cassie. "You're all set, sweetheart. God worked it out; now the country club *does* fit your budget."

Cassie burst into tears of relief and gratitude. My mom went over to her on the couch and put her arm around her, asking me to get some tissues. I passed a few her way, and while Cassie dried her eyes, my dad came over and gave her a hug, too.

"I don't know how Brian and I can ever thank you, Mr. Duncan. You've just given us a fairy-tale wedding; it's a Cinderella story in every way. If you've ever been in Keldon's, you know it's *nothing* like the country club.

"It's funny; I'm not even sure why I came here tonight. There didn't seem to be a fix to my problem, but I just felt like I was supposed to stop by and talk to you about it. It's not nice to say, but now I'm almost glad Keldon's burned down."

We all laughed despite ourselves. Then my mom spoke next. "You can be sure God didn't cause the fire at Keldon's for you Cassie, but He did take a terrible situation and turn it around to benefit you. It's no coincidence that the only place in town with a cancellation on your wedding day was the country club where we had special favor with the owner. Because God knows everything in advance, He had already made a provision for your need before it ever came up. Think about it: my husband earned a favor from Calvin last year, and the booking at the country club was cancelled before the fire this morning."

"That's true, Mrs. Duncan. We serve such a wonderful God!"

"You played a part in what happened tonight, too, Cassie."

"What do you mean?"

"Living as a Christian is about learning how to be led by God's Spirit. What if you hadn't followed that prompting from the Lord to come over here tonight and share your problem? If you'd stayed at home, feeling sorry for yourself and accepting your situation as unsolvable, you could have missed this opportunity to be blessed. Someone else could've booked the country club by the time we learned about Keldon's."

Wide-eyed, Cassie admitted, "You're right! I never thought of that. Oh, I can't wait to tell Brian! Do you mind if I call him on my cell really quick?"

"Of course not! Go into my husband's study."

As I waited for Cassie to finish her call, I was overwhelmed with gratitude for what God had just done for my best friend. I silently thanked Him: *Father, Brian and Cassie don't come from wealthy families, and this kind of reception would've been impossible for them on their incomes. I feel like You're giving them this beautiful reception as a reward for years of faithfulness to You and to others. Certainly, they are two of the kindest, most caring people around, and I'm proud to be one of their closest friends. Thanks for taking such good care of them!*

After talking with Brian, Cassie almost skipped out of the study to thank my parents again. Excited to go home and share the good news with her family, she left right away.

I was feeling tired by now; it had been a long day. After saying good night to my mom and dad, I went directly to my room and got ready to go to sleep.

Before getting into bed, I went over to my keepsake box and read David's card one more time. Then I turned out the light and scooted underneath the covers.

Moonlight was streaming through the French doors of my balcony, and I could see the silhouette of my daisies across the room. With a happy sigh, I fell asleep, a hopeful smile still on my face.

Chapter 6

The Other Woman

Arriving at the Center early the next day, I finished up some paperwork and began my morning rehab appointments. By lunchtime, I was more than ready for a break. Grabbing my sack lunch, I headed to the staff lounge.

While I was finishing my sandwich, Miss Lottie came in looking for me. Happy to see her again, I gave her a welcome-back hug, and she joined me at my table. As I filled her in on all the latest news, I noticed she wasn't her usual, inquisitive self. Something was wrong.

Before I had a chance to ask, she explained. "I'm about to undergo a big change, Julia. Now that my sister has had this stroke, she has a long recovery ahead of her. She has other health issues that require her to stay where she is in a dry climate. Deirdre and I have always been good friends; now she needs me.

There isn't anybody else to take care of her, so I'm giving up my apartment next door and moving out there to be with her."

"When will that be?" I asked, sadly.

"She's getting out of the hospital in a week. That means I only have a few days to pack my things, sell or give away what I can't take, and settle into her place in time to bring her home."

"How am I going to get along without you, Miss Lottie? You're one of my closest friends."

"I'll miss you, too, dear, but I'm needed elsewhere. You and I have made a good team telling people here at the Center about Christ. But from what you tell me, I won't be leaving you alone. You can join forces with that handsome new doctor you've met. He'd make a good partner for you, don't you think?"

I didn't respond to her last statement, knowing exactly what she was implying. Instead, I gave her a hug and made her promise to come over to the Center and see me as often as possible before she left.

After lunch, I worked with several different residents before leaving for the day around four o'clock. Walking out of the Center into the fresh air, the beautiful weather invited me to stay outdoors. With a little time before my evening class, I decided to head to the park for a while. Quickly retracing my steps into the building, I bought some peanuts from the cafeteria vending machine. As I was leaving the second time, Miss Lottie was in the lobby, talking to a resident.

"Where are you off to this lovely day?" she inquired.

I held up the bag of nuts. "Murphy's Landing to feed the squirrels."

"Have a nice time," she called to me as I walked out the door.

When I got into my car, I called David on his cell. He took Thursday afternoons off, so I knew I wouldn't be interrupting him with a patient. He answered on the second ring.

"Hi, David. It's Julia."

"Oh, hi," he answered, somewhat distracted.

"I just got off work and wanted to call and thank you for the daisies. That was really thoughtful of you."

"Glad you liked them," he replied, his voice trailing off. "Not now—I'm on the phone," he playfully scolded someone with him. Laughing, he turned his attention to me again. "Sorry, Julia. My running partner is getting impatient to get going; she and I were about to leave when you called."

"Sounds like this is a bad time, David. Have a good run," I pushed out before hanging up abruptly. Immediately, I turned off my phone. I didn't want to talk to anyone.

"How stupid can I be?" I cried inwardly, flushing with embarrassment. "Obviously, someone else is in his condo. I should have known I'm not the only woman he spends time with!"

All sorts of emotions instantly surged through me. I felt shocked, hurt, disappointed, and betrayed. There was no justifiable reason for me to feel that way, but I couldn't help it. I was ashamed to admit it, but I was jealous.

I didn't want to go to the park anymore. Everything in me wanted to find some private place to have a good cry. Even so, I started my car and headed to the park anyway. I would not act like a silly schoolgirl. I could handle this.

As I drove, a real sense of loss came over me. It was like I'd been straining for so long to reach a certain point, to finally be at the brink of a meaningful relationship, only to be suddenly pushed back to square one—to nothing special at all. I kept thinking how I really didn't need this. My life was stressful enough with work and school.

I was glad when I finally reached Murphy's Landing. Finding a spot close to the pier, I parked my car and grabbed the package of peanuts off the front seat.

It was a perfect April day; the sun felt warm and soothing as I made my way to a favorite bench near a small cluster of oak trees. My furry friends were already there, racing up and down the nearby tree trunks. Their antics almost made me crack a smile as I watched them play. Almost.

I'd spent many afternoons on this bench after work, throwing peanuts to the squirrels, drinking in the peace and quiet of the park, trying to de-stress between my shift at the Center and class. I doubted it would make me feel better today. Momentarily, I stopped throwing nuts and closed my eyes. I could see David's face, and I found myself wishing he were sitting beside me.

"Those peanuts any good?" a voice unexpectedly asked, interrupting my thoughts. I opened my eyes in surprise, looking from side to side, but the voice had apparently come from directly behind me. Turning, I found David looking down at me, grinning.

"You weren't easy to find, you know," he said, leaning down beside me, over the back of the bench. "Good thing I'm a great detective."

"How did you know I was here?"

"You weren't answering your cell, so I stopped by the Center on the off chance Miss Lottie was around. You said she'd be back today. I found her in the lobby, and here I am."

"I thought you had plans with a friend," I responded, coolly.

"I do," he admitted, unaffected. "Can't you tell?" He was referring to his running outfit. I actually resented him for looking so handsome in only sweats and a T-shirt.

"We stopped here first because I wanted you to meet my running partner," he said, straightening up. "I'm sure you'll like her."

Managing *not* to roll my eyes, I gave him a forced smile. Meeting the other woman did not appeal to me at all, but I didn't seem to have a choice in the matter. Looking around, I asked, "Where is she?"

"In the car, waiting. I wasn't sure you would be here, so I came on ahead to check. We're going jogging, you know."

"Yes, I remember," I answered, trying to hide my jealousy.

"Wait here, then. I'll go get her."

While he returned to his car, I leaned back against the bench, closed my eyes, and tried to mentally prepare myself. I wanted to be gracious when I met this woman; I had no right to dislike her. I couldn't understand why David was so eager for us to meet. Surely, he must have known how awkward this was going to be. At first, I was irritated with Miss Lottie for telling David where I was. Then I decided it was better for me to find out where I stood with him before our relationship went any further.

Something cold and wet brushed my arm, startling me. Opening my eyes, I saw a large golden retriever staring up at me. "Hello there," I responded, temporarily forgetting my troubles. Reaching out to pet the dog, I added, "You sure are friendly."

"She is."

That was the second time David had stolen up on me undetected. Smiling, he said, "I see you've met my running partner. Julia, this is Sandy."

Instantly, all the anxiety I had been battling since our phone conversation vanished. I'm sure my facial expression was an open window to my soul. Grinning at David from ear to ear, I couldn't hide my feelings of elation. *This* was the other female in David's life? Needless to say, I immediately loved that dog!

By now, David was sitting beside me on the bench petting Sandy, too. For the next few minutes, she became our focus. We both knew I had unfairly judged him, but he didn't bring that up. It was clear his motivation for finding me so quickly had been totally unselfish—not to vindicate himself, but to relieve my anxious feelings and protect our growing friendship. He was intentionally trying to spare me any embarrassment. For him, it appeared to be enough that I'd come to know the truth.

"How long have you had Sandy?" I eventually asked.

"Almost three years. I had a golden retriever growing up, and I missed having one when I was in college and med school. Once I started interning, I decided to invest in a dog again. She ties me down in a lot of ways, but she's worth it."

"I love dogs. Our family hasn't had one for a few years, though. Our standard poodle had to be put to sleep, and my dad felt that with their busy schedule, John being married, and me in school, a new dog wouldn't get much attention."

Finding the peanut bag on the bench, Sandy started sniffing at it. David reprimanded her. "No, girl. Your treats are at home."

"Want some?" I asked, holding out the bag to him.

"No, I'm fine. But I think your friends would like some more. Look over there." Two squirrels were peeking out from behind a nearby tree, reluctant to come any closer because of Sandy.

"Oh, you mean Tom and Jerry."

David shook his head. "You might want to rename the little one Geraldine."

"Is that your professional observation as a doctor?"

"Nope, just a hunch. They look like a couple to me."

Sandy had moved over by David and was nudging him. "Okay, girl. I promised you a good run. You've been very patient."

"I've got to leave anyway, David. I need to go home and change before class tonight."

Getting up, he said, "I've got a court reserved for next Wednesday if you want to play."

I smiled and nodded *yes*. David and Sandy walked me back to my car and then left to get some exercise. Unfortunately, the only exercise I'd gotten that day was jumping to conclusions. As I drove home, I repented for my foolishness.

Father, I'm so embarrassed about how quick I was to think bad of David, that he was leading me on while spending time with some other woman. Please forgive me for acting self-centeredly, for hanging up on him so rudely! I will never again convict David on circumstantial evidence. If I'd simply stayed on the phone and acted like a reasonable person, this misunderstanding wouldn't have happened!

I'm grateful this all worked out, that David was willing to come after me to explain. How romantic that was! But more than anything, the way David handled this shows me that my feelings are important to him, even more important, perhaps, than his own. It must have hurt him when I hung up like I did, so quick to believe the worst. He deserves better, and I promise to always believe the best of David. Thank You for patiently working with me, Lord! Help me to be as

good a friend to David as he has been to me. And if You
do have a future for me with this amazing guy, Lord,
so be it!

When I got home, I chatted with my mom for a
few minutes, changed my clothes, and breezed out
again, taking a sandwich with me to eat on the way. I
liked my Thursday night class; my professor was one
of the best in her field. Still, I was longing for summer
break just a few months off.

When I got home that night, I checked my email.
There were two new messages. The first one was
from a girl in my church group asking about an
upcoming youth event. I answered it right away. The
second was from Paul:

Hey, Julia.

I miss being with you a lot, and I think you know
my feelings for you haven't changed. That's why
I acted the way I did in Benny's the other day.
Sorry if I embarrassed you. It's hard to be patient
when you care so much about someone. I keep
waiting and hoping you'll come to your senses
and see the light about us—a green light, that
is. It seems like every time I see you lately, that
doctor is with you. Please don't tell me you're
falling for that guy! You don't know anything
about him. Have you forgotten how much fun we
used to have together? How we both felt when
I kissed you? Let me take you out to dinner on
Saturday night so we can talk, okay?

Reading his message, I couldn't help but sigh in
frustration. How was I going to get him to understand there was no future for us? Why couldn't he

just accept it and find someone else? I answered his email with just one word—**NO!** As I hit the *send* button, I felt an initial surge of guilt. I hated to be insensitive to anyone, but I was worn out explaining to Paul over and over why I couldn't return his love.

I opened my Bible and read for a while before getting ready for bed. Crawling under my comforter, I leaned back into my pillow and settled into a comfortable position. *Father, I only have two requests tonight. Please let Paul pass his CPA exam next month, and please make him see that I'm never going to change my mind about him!*

Paul was a groomsman in Brian and Cassie's wedding, so he would naturally be in Weston until July. But once the wedding was over, with me out of the picture, there wouldn't be any reason for him to stay here anymore. It would finally be over. As I fell asleep that night, I completely underestimated what Paul would do to keep David and me apart.

Dinner and a Movie

I awoke the next morning refreshed by the extra hours of sleep Friday mornings allowed. I didn't have to be at the Center until ten. With my incredibly full schedule, those two additional hours were heaven!

My parents were already at the firm, and it was Kitty's day off, leaving me to fend for myself. Once I was showered and ready for work, I ate breakfast at my computer, answering questions from my girls in the youth program. Finishing up, I went down to the kitchen and packed a lunch before leaving for work.

My rehab sessions were more of a challenge on Fridays because many of the female residents were getting their hair done at the Center's beauty shop, requiring me to work my schedule around their appointments. I didn't see Miss Lottie all day. I figured she was busy next door, packing.

When my shift was over, I signed out and walked to my car. As I unlocked the door, David pulled in alongside me in his car and lowered the window. "Hey, Julia. I was hoping to catch you before you left. I'm on my way to the hospital. Where are you off to?"

"Just home."

"Got anything planned for tonight?"

"Not yet."

"Good. I had a meeting scheduled with Dr. Feinberg, but he called and postponed it until tomorrow. So, I'm free for the night. How does dinner and a movie sound?"

"Great! What time?"

"Six o'clock?"

"That works for me."

"Okay, I'll be at your house around six. Dress casual."

"All right. See you soon."

I was about to turn and head for my car when he said, "Wait, I almost forgot. I've got something for you." Then he passed a coffee cup through the open window. "I stopped for a cappuccino on my way over and thought you might like one."

"Oh, thanks. I could use a pick-me-up," I replied, taking it from him.

Driving home, I was floating on air, ecstatic to actually have a Friday night date. I didn't know where we were eating or what movies were playing, but it didn't matter. I was going to be with David again, and all I could think of was what I should wear.

A few minutes later, I pulled into our garage, parked my car, and walked into the kitchen where my mother was preparing dinner. She could tell I was on cloud nine about something.

"What are you drinking?" she asked, watching me finish off the cup David had given me. When I told her what it was, she broke out in a delighted smile. I could read her thoughts: This was the first cappuccino I had been able to drink since my last date with Jay. My mom once said she would know for sure that I'd been healed from the trauma of that horrible night when she saw me drinking one again.

Announcing I wouldn't be eating at home and why, I ran upstairs to pick out an outfit. My bed soon became overrun with rejects. Eventually, I decided on what I thought looked best. As I congratulated myself on my final selection, I glanced at the clock. It was already four-fifty! I didn't realize I'd spent so much time trying on clothes. I only had a little over an hour to shower and look stunning by six.

Throwing myself into high gear, I did my best to be ready on time. I missed the mark by ten minutes. When I walked downstairs, David had already arrived and was sitting in the living room, talking with my parents.

"You look nice," he said, standing as I entered the room.

"Thanks. Sorry I'm a little late."

"We're okay on time. I made the reservation for six-thirty. The restaurant isn't far from here; if we leave now, we'll be fine."

We said a quick goodbye to my parents and left right away. David walked me to the passenger side of his car and opened the door. A Frisbee was lying on my seat. He picked it up and tossed it in the back. "That's Sandy's," he explained, grinning. I smiled back at him. As David helped me into the car, our eyes met, sending an unspoken message: everything was better when we were together.

"Do you like Thai food?" he asked once we were underway.

"Love it, especially pad thai."

"Me, too. I thought we'd check out the new place on Marshall Street."

"You mean Celestial Gardens? I haven't been there yet, but Cassie and Brian said it was great."

There was a long line when we arrived at the restaurant; I was glad David had made reservations. After a slight wait, the hostess led us to a private little table on an outside wall. The Asian décor and peaceful water fountains strategically placed throughout the dining area created the perfect setting for our first dinner date.

Scanning the menu, David started us with a satay appetizer, and we each ordered the chicken pad thai. As we waited for the food to come, curiosity prompted me to ask David why he had decided to set up his practice so far away from his home in Baymont.

"Actually, it's because Dr. Feinberg has his offices here."

"I've never met Dr. Feinberg. He hasn't been in Weston very long himself, has he?"

"Only two years or so. I first heard about him from another intern at the hospital in Baymont. He asked me to go with him to a natural medicine seminar where Dr. Feinberg was speaking. What he said at that meeting changed my life—personally and professionally."

Our conversation was interrupted by the arrival of our appetizer. Once David had prayed over the food, I asked him to tell me what Dr. Feinberg said that was so life changing. He explained while we were eating.

"It was such an amazing night, Julia. He started out by recapping the first fifteen years of his career as a traditional physician. He said that after he had done his best to diagnose his patients' illnesses, he routinely wrote out prescriptions for them. After years of treating people this way, he noticed that although the drugs offered some immediate relief, many also caused serious side effects.

"When he was about forty-five, he met several doctors who had incorporated natural medicine into their practices and were seeing incredible results. They mentored him, and now he's training men and women all over the world to use diet, lifestyle changes, and natural methods to treat their patients instead of simply using drugs. Dr. Feinberg's really balanced, though. He'll prescribe a drug when it's needed, but he sees the use of drugs as a short-term answer to an immediate problem, with the goal of replacing them with a more natural remedy as soon as possible."

Again we were interrupted when the waitress brought our entrées. The spicy seasoning on the pad thai was perfect. David suggested I try some of the peanut sauce on the table. It was delicious. Getting back to our conversation, I said, "I can see why you found the seminar so interesting."

David continued, "But the most important part came after Dr. Feinberg spoke. He had three former patients come on stage and share how his methods had helped to cure them of diseases. The first two testimonies were inspiring, but it was the third that struck a nerve.

"The woman's name was Allison, and she had been diagnosed as a teenager with the same kind of cancer as my sister, Carrie. Her doctors prescribed the traditional battery of tests and treatments, offering no real hope for survival. Fortunately, her parents heard about Dr. Feinberg and the success he was having with cancer patients. They decided to pursue natural methods with their daughter as well. Today she is cancer-free and enjoying a healthy and active life.

"Sitting there listening to Allison's story, I had to fight back tears, Julia. My heart was crying out for my sister, but she was gone, and there was nothing I could do to bring her back. I decided then to dedicate my life to all the other Carries who could still be helped."

The look in his eyes showed that David had made more than just a decision that night; God had placed a divine call on his life. When I told him that, he agreed. "You know when God has told you to do something because no matter how many discouragements or obstacles you encounter, you can't quit."

"So, how did you end up getting connected with Dr. Feinberg?"

"It was the favor of God, Julia. I went up after the meeting and waited in a long line to talk to him. I told him that I wanted to study under him and why. He's a Christian, too. He said several times at the seminar that faith and prayer were two of the most essential parts of the healing process. I told him I was a Christian, and we hit it off right away.

"The following week, he checked my credentials at the hospital and met me for lunch. He explained that he was moving his practice to Weston to be closer to his grandchildren. He wanted to work with like-minded doctors, and he asked me to come to Weston once my internship was over and join his medical group. And here I am."

"I admire you for having the courage to make that decision, David. Natural medicine isn't always recognized as credible by some doctors, is it?"

"No. Sometimes physicians who incorporate natural treatments or chiropractic adjustments into their practices are labeled as unprofessional. That doesn't bother me as long as I can provide my patients with a safe and lasting way to regain their health. The recovery statistics for natural medicine are out there for anyone who has an open mind."

"Your parents must be very proud of you."

"My dad is, but my mother thinks I'm a fool. She had her heart set on me staying in Baymont and setting up my practice among all her country club friends."

"You haven't talked much about your parents. What do they do?"

"My dad's a banker, and my mother runs several charities in Baymont, entertains a lot, things like that." Stopping to check his watch, David announced that we needed to go to make it to the theater in time. Spying our server, he quickly got her attention and paid the bill.

Making it to the movie theater with a few minutes to spare, we stopped at the concession counter. After a few moments of deliberation, we decided to share some popcorn and a big box of candy.

The movie ended up being very funny. I would never have predicted such a crazy ending! David and I laughed so hard, I was wiping away tears at the credits. And there was no relief on the drive home as we reviewed scenes that started us laughing all over again. I couldn't remember having this much fun with anyone.

Once we turned into my neighborhood, I started to get a little nervous, wondering how we would say good night. I wasn't sure what to expect as we pulled into my driveway.

Shutting off the motor, David got out, went around to open my door, and helped me out of the car. Then he escorted me up the front steps. Reaching for my hand, he gave it an affectionate squeeze. "I had a really good time tonight, Julia."

"Me, too. Thanks for such a nice evening."

"We'll do it again soon. I'll see you in church Sunday."

"See you then."

As it turned out, saying good night hadn't been awkward at all. When David reached the bottom of the stairs, he turned around again. "By the way, I've been approved to take that boys' group at church."

"Great! There's a leaders' meeting this Tuesday night."

"I know; Pastor Kevin told me. I'll be there."

When he was out of earshot, I mumbled, "Paul will be there, too. I hope he behaves himself."

Letting myself in the front door, I headed straight upstairs to my room. My parents were already in bed, so I tried to be quiet as I walked through the dark hallway.

Before going to sleep, I read several verses from my Bible and journaled about my date with David for a few minutes. Then I offered up a short prayer: *Thank You, Father, for sending such a wonderful man into my life. I don't know what the future holds for us, Lord. I only know I'm loving the present!*

A Happier Melody

For as long as I could remember, Sunday mornings had an unchanging routine: waking up early, getting showered and dressed, eating a quick breakfast, and hurrying to leave the house on time for church. For me, something new had been added to the mix: trying to look my best for David.

Paul was at church early the Sunday morning after my dinner date with David, talking to one of the boys from his group. Once my parents and I were seated, he walked down the aisle and sat with us. As we made small talk, David arrived. My heart sank when he saw Paul sitting next to me. I hadn't asked Paul to join us, but David didn't know that. I expected him to shy away from the situation by finding a seat somewhere else, but he didn't. He walked right up to us and extended his hand to my parents.

"Good morning, Mr. Duncan, Mrs. Duncan. Hi Julia, Paul. Mind if I join you today?"

Paul shot him a look of disapproval as he reluctantly shook the hand now extended to him. "Sure, Dr. Stanton. Oh, sorry," he added in a patronizing tone. "You like to be called David, I hear."

"By my friends," David responded, grinning as he sat down beside my father. "Not everyone wants to be a friend, though, do they?"

My dad noticed Paul's annoyed expression and quickly changed the subject. The church service was uncomfortable from that point on as Paul sat close to me, glancing my way continually, acting as though we had come to church together as a couple. Of course, his act was for David's benefit.

Before the sermon ended, David's cell started vibrating, and he had to excuse himself to go to the hospital. I could tell Paul was happy when David had to leave. When the service was over, Paul asked me to have lunch with him somewhere so we could talk. I grabbed his arm, pulling him to a private corner in the back of the church.

Angry, I asked, "Didn't you get my reply to your email?"

"Yes," he answered, apprehensively.

"Then you know my answer about lunch today! I don't love you, Paul. And from the way you're acting, I'm starting to not even like you!"

"I can thank David for that," he spat.

"No, you get all the credit. The way you treat David just shows me that you're *not* the kind of man I want to spend the rest of my life with. Any doubts

I may have had about you are gone. Stop punishing David because I don't want to be with you!"

"But you don't mind being with *him*, right?"

"My private life is none of your business, Paul. Just ask yourself whether you still want us to be friends. Because if you can't act like an adult, I'm done with our friendship. Think it over," I said sharply before turning and walking away.

My parents took me out to lunch that afternoon. When we got to the restaurant, I filled them in on what had happened with Paul. They approved of the way I had handled him. My father didn't appreciate Paul's possessiveness toward me, saying he'd step in and have a talk with him if Paul didn't stop. My dad didn't say so, but I could tell he was pulling for David. They got along well, and that meant a lot to me.

The next week was extremely busy. On Monday, the Center had a going-away party for Miss Lottie. We both cried when we said goodbye, promising to keep in touch.

Tuesday night was our leaders' meeting at church. There, Paul announced that he was taking his CPA exam in a week and asked everyone to keep praying for him. His behavior toward David and me wasn't very friendly, but he wasn't rude either. I was hopeful he was finally beginning to face reality.

David and I played racquetball again on Wednesday afternoon. What a great guy! I love his laugh, and he laughed often. He made me laugh, too. I found myself continually looking forward to the next time we would be together.

Both of us were busy people, however. David was studying with Dr. Feinberg after hours, and I was working at the Center and finishing up my first semester of grad school. Yet no matter how demanding our schedules became, we managed to steal a few hours away to play racquetball, grab a quick lunch, or take in a movie.

Meanwhile, my prayers for Paul were finally answered: he had passed his CPA exam. Not everyone passes every part the first time. I was thrilled for him *and* for me. Maybe now he would start making plans to go home.

Spring gradually turned into summer, and I purposely signed up for only two classes. I was anxious to get my master's degree as quickly as possible, but I also wanted to have more free time to be with David. I was never happier than when I was with him. He gave every indication of feeling the same about me.

So far, our relationship had remained as friends. David hadn't kissed me or said he loved me yet. Holding back from romance for the moment was giving us the chance to build something stronger than romantic feelings alone, something more lasting. It gave me breathing room to get to know and appreciate the real David without pressure, without the fear of repeating my mistakes with Jay.

Brian and Cassie's wedding was rapidly approaching. The way things worked out, I was spending less time with David and more with Cassie, helping her to get ready for her big day. In mid-June, Cassie and Brian had a beautiful bridal shower at our church.

As her maid of honor, my time was divided between working on that and planning her personal shower.

When my dress for Cassie's wedding finally came in, there had been a mix up on the color, and it was too late to reorder. Fortunately, the bridal shop had one like it in stock, only two sizes larger. The seamstress who did the alterations assured me she could easily take it in for me. Four fittings later, she was still making adjustments. Cassie was thankful the store hadn't made the same mistake with the bridesmaid dresses for her three sisters.

Brian's older brother, James, was going to be his best man. Paul, Cassie's brother, Todd, and one of Brian's friends from law school completed the wedding party—with two adorable little cousins as the flower girl and ring bearer, of course.

The future Mr. and Mrs. Douglas had done a wonderful job of planning their wedding, keeping it simple but elegant, with stress levels at a minimum. While other engaged couples I knew seemed upset with each other much of the time, Brian and Cassie were having fun planning their wedding together. They were setting a much better example, and I was taking notes.

Flip and Melody were planning their wedding at the same time. That meant I was also spending a lot of afternoons with Melody, helping her to find the perfect gown and pick out dresses for the bridesmaids. She was such a sweetheart, the ideal girl for Flip. I first met her when she started coming to church with him. Gradually, we became friends, meeting for coffee sometimes between work and classes. I was honored when Melody asked me to be a bridesmaid.

I think I first noticed a change in her attitude toward me around the end of June. It was one of those things I couldn't really put my finger on, nothing she actually said or did. But there it was, nevertheless, just under the surface whenever we were together. I could feel it when Melody talked to me, see it in her eyes when we'd go out with David and Flip.

I prayed about it for a while before saying anything to her. Feeling awkward about bringing it up, I was waiting for the right time and place. My opportunity came, oddly enough, the day of Cassie's personal shower. Melody had offered to bake a cake for the party, and I had asked her to drop it off at my house a few hours early so I could use it as a centerpiece for the food table.

When Melody arrived, we carried the cake into the family room and set it on the table. Melody had done an amazing job; it was simply elegant, exceeding my expectations. I complimented her on how lovely it was as I positioned it exactly where I wanted. Expecting to see a smile when I turned to her, I was surprised to find Melody on the verge of tears.

"Are you okay?" I asked, wondering if this might be a good time to ask her what had been going on lately. When she shrugged off my question without answering, I knew it was. "Melody, I've been feeling tension between us for weeks. Please tell me what's bothering you. Have I done or said something to hurt you?"

That was all it took. Instantly, a flood of tears came streaming out, as though they'd been dammed up and couldn't be held back any longer. I reached for some tissues on a nearby end table and invited Melody to come talk with me on the couch. Once we sat down, she confessed that she'd been fighting resentment about Flip and me.

"Flip and me?" I reacted, shocked. "Melody, what are you talking about? Flip and I are friends, nothing more."

"Now maybe, but what about before?"

"Before what?" I asked, bewildered.

"Before he started dating me. I found out you broke up with him the year before I met him."

"Melody, Flip and I never dated. Who in the world told you that?"

"Jeremy from church. Remember the softball tournament a few weeks ago?"

"Sure, I had to leave early because of work."

"Well, Flip was at bat when you were going, and I saw you cheer for him on the way to your car. Jeremy was sitting next to me on the bleachers, icing a pulled muscle. I said something to him about you being such a good friend. Jeremy looked surprised and said it wasn't always that way, that Flip had been totally in love with you once. He said a few more things about you breaking Flip's heart and then climbed down the bleachers to sit with the rest of the players again. I was numb, realizing I'd gotten Flip on the rebound. He couldn't get you, so he settled for me."

"That's not true, Melody," I assured her. "Have you talked to Flip about this?"

"He didn't tell me the truth about you before, Julia. Why would he admit it now?"

"Because Flip's one of the most honest people I know! He's an open book; you know that. Listen, Melody, when I met Flip, he was totally different from what he's like now. Not to be mean, but he was kind of annoying, having no real plans for a career, talking nonstop, and rarely listening to anyone else.

"I first met him at Weston U. Shortly after that, Jeremy started bringing him to the singles' group. At the time, I was the only one he knew at those meetings besides Jeremy. It's true he had a crush on me for a while and did a lot of talking about how he felt about me, but I eventually talked to him about it and told him I didn't like him as a boyfriend. And that was the end of it.

"Trust me, Melody, he wasn't in love with me. I was just one of the first girls at college he got to know. You are the love of his life. Don't *ever* doubt that. Like I said, Flip isn't even the same person he was when he liked me; he's really changed. He's learned who he is in Christ and what he really wants in life. And he wants *you*. You're not second choice for Flip, Melody. You're *God's choice* for Flip. Ugh, I could kick Jeremy for opening his big mouth the way he did! I don't know what he was thinking. I hope you feel better now that you know the truth."

The smile on her face indicated she did. "I still don't understand why Flip never told me about all this, Julia."

"I guess there wasn't any reason to. I mean, have you told Flip about all your old crushes?"

"No, I guess not."

"See? What's most important is what has happened since you started dating each other. A girl I work with at the Center found out her fiancé had been engaged before her. She was so disappointed to think of him proposing to someone else; she'd wanted to be his first and only love. I reminded her that a lot of people don't get to the altar without first making some mistakes. One day I'll have to tell my future husband about what happened to me with Jay. If he truly loves me, it won't make any difference."

"This whole thing was pretty dumb, wasn't it, Julia? I'm sorry for the way I've been acting around you."

"Don't worry about it, Melody. I'm just glad we talked about what was bothering you. My friendship with you and Flip is important to me; I don't want to lose it."

"Neither do I," she sighed. "Well, I'd better get going. I'm meeting Flip for lunch downtown. Thanks for being so understanding."

I walked her to the door and said goodbye. "See you in a couple hours," I called out as she headed toward her car. She wasn't the only one relieved after our talk. I was glad a happier Melody would be coming to the party that night. Before getting into the shower a few hours later, I got an unexpected call.

"Julia, it's Flip."

"Hi," I replied, surprised to hear from him.

"Just wanna say thanks."

"For what?"

"For whatever you an' Melody talked about today. She said she stopped by your place before meetin' me for lunch and ya cleared up some stuff, whatever that means. She's been actin' funny for a couple weeks, but wouldn't tell me why. Now she's her ol' self again. What'd ya say, anyway? She wouldn't tell me."

"Just girl talk, that's all."

"Huh?" he asked, puzzled.

"You know, Flip, stuff we talk about that you men don't get."

"Like now, I'm thinkin'."

"Exactly. Well, I've got to get ready for Cassie's shower, more exciting girl speak on the way..."

"Yeah, bye, Julia," he replied, apparently happy our confusing conversation was over.

I was laughing when I stepped into the shower. There's just something about keeping guys guessing that makes being a girl so much fun!

Tradition

When my mom came home from the office, she helped me get the rest of the food ready for Cassie's shower. I loved being in the kitchen with my mom; she was quite the chef and always made cooking fun. Kitty cooked at our house a lot, too. Working alongside both of them, I'd learned to make some salads and desserts, but I'd never made an entire dinner from start to finish.

Lately, I had been trying to pay more attention when my mom was preparing main dishes. I hadn't cared to learn before, but I started to realize that once I was married, my husband might appreciate having home-cooked meals, and my culinary skills were pretty sorry. I had always assumed I could learn to be a good cook *after* I got married, but I didn't really want my husband to start off our married life as my guinea pig, with his first few meals from me sad burnt offerings. I had recently written some goals for my life in my journal. One of them was to prepare myself to be a great wife for my Mr. Right. Improving my cooking skills was an easy way to start.

A few weeks before, my grandmother had spoken at a ladies' meeting and said several things about marriage which I recorded in my journal later. She talked about the dynamics of marriage, how it's a beautiful relationship of give and take, that it's like a right and left hand working together, each doing its part, each providing its own strength and finesse.

She went on to say, "God created men to be appetite driven in every area of their lives: spirit, soul, and body. That's what gives them the motivation they need to lead their homes spiritually, work hard to provide for their families, and procreate future generations. A wise wife understands how ingrained those traits are in her man, how important all three areas are to him. She makes it a point to minister to her husband in each one. That means loving him enough to let him lead the home spiritually, even if he doesn't do it exactly how she would. She lets him be who he is as one hand while coming alongside as the other hand to bring whatever else is needed.

"It also means taking the time and effort to make your home a peaceful place to retreat to after struggling all day to make a living. You both may have jobs and will need to work together to find balance, but your man needs you to run the house in a way that makes all your hard work together worth it. Never underestimate the value of great meals and quality time spent together in an orderly, peaceful home. The effort you make to create that atmosphere will go a long way in letting your man know how much he's worth to you!

"Lastly, you want to be a wise wife who understands how important the sexual relationship is to your husband. It's you he's working so hard for, it's you he's choosing to be faithful to, and it's you he wants to make proud. But if you rarely want to have sex with your husband, *it's you he feels he has failed.*"

I had never thought about sex that way, about how important it is to a man's psyche. I just figured once the romance of being a newlywed wore off, it was more physical than anything, a *need*, as the saying goes. I hadn't realized it meant so much to a man emotionally to have his wife desire and enjoy the sexual part of their relationship, too.

Obviously, I couldn't work on this area with my Mr. Right until *after* we were married, but listening to my grandmother's message made me value it even more as a beautiful part of what we would have together. I saw that I would need to make sex a priority after I was married, to always respect how much it meant to my man, to reward him for choosing to keep himself faithful to me. How good God is to make something so necessary so enjoyable!

Toward the end of her talk, my grandma brought up the other *"s"* word in marriage, the one some people consider an obsolete word these days: *submission*. What my grandma said that night was more or less what my mom had explained to me years before, but the way my grandma painted the picture for us made the concept even clearer for me.

Surprisingly, my grandma didn't start with any traditional submission scriptures, but instead began with the Love Chapter in 1 Corinthians 13. She read verses 4-8 from the Amplified version, and I wrote down the following lines from those verses:

> "Love endures long and is patient and kind...it is not rude (unmannerly) and does not act unbecomingly. Love (God's love in us) does not insist on its own rights or its own way, for it is not self-seeking...it is not touchy or fretful or resentful... love bears up under anything and everything that comes, is ever ready to believe the best of every person, its hopes are fadeless under all circumstances, and it endures everything [without weakening]. Love never fails..."

My grandma reminded us that these verses were written for *both* husbands and wives to live out. Then she read the famous scriptures regarding submission found in Ephesians chapter 5. She started with verse 21 where all Christians were given an instruction: "Submit to one another out of reverence for Christ."

She explained that this applies to marriage as well. We are supposed to submit to one another in life, giving and taking, working together smoothly like a right and left hand, putting those verses about love into action. And why? Because we're respecting Christ. We don't prefer each other as husband and wife because we always feel like it or want to; we put the other person first because Christ put our needs ahead of His own when He went to the cross. Out of our respect for Him, we respect each other. Period.

What a refreshing perspective! When we respect and honor one another with God's love, motivated by our respect for Christ, we won't take advantage of each other. Instead, we will cherish what each one of us brings to the table.

Then she read the rest of that chapter from the New Living Translation, verses 22-33. I wrote down the following lines from what she read:

> "For wives, this means submit to your husbands as to the Lord. For a husband is the head of his wife as Christ is the head of the church. He is the Savior of his body, the church. As the church submits to Christ, so you wives should submit to your husbands in everything. For husbands, this means love your wives, just as Christ loved the church. He gave up his life for her...In the same way, husbands ought to love their wives as they love their own bodies. For a man who loves his wife actually shows love for himself...each man must love his wife as he loves himself, and the wife must respect her husband."

My grandma told us that *respect* is what is most important to the heart of a man. The way God created him, it's respect which makes him feel truly valued and loved. Your choice to respect him makes him feel like you trust him, that he can accomplish anything in life with you by his side, that he can be the man God created him to be, someone actually worth something and worthy of your love.

She also explained that *love* is the most important thing to the heart of a woman. It makes her feel valued and appreciated as a true treasure, the best thing that's ever happened to her husband. And this love ushers in honor and respect as well. No abuse. No disrespect. Just love and the realization that you are pursuing God's perfect will for your lives and your family together as a team. She said these Bible verses were written to teach us, whether husband or wife, how to give what our spouse needs the most in marriage.

Wow! I had never thought of it that way. In fact, it struck me that the husband's requirement is actually pretty difficult: he is supposed to love his wife *like Christ loves His Church!* Since Jesus literally died for us, there is a lot expected of a husband's love for his wife, loving her sacrificially, just as much as he loves himself.

That eliminates the wrong notion that a wife can be mistreated or ordered around in a demeaning way, like she were a child who must obey. That's not what God is talking about in those verses. Jesus doesn't boss, belittle, or abuse us, so neither does a good man his wife. Jesus treasures His Bride, the Church, and so should a husband treasure the beautiful and capable wife God has given him.

My grandma taught us that our part as a wife includes supporting our husband by respecting him as the God-established leader of the home. It's not that we don't have any say or input. On the contrary, like a partnership that requires equal investment, effort, and communication, so our husband needs our sensitivity, creativity, perspective, and counsel as we make decisions for the home together. We provide pieces to the puzzle that are indispensible!

Yet when all is said and done and we cannot come to a place of agreement, we yield so a decision can be made and our unit can move forward in peace and respect. Submitting means *choosing to yield* for the sake of peace—and doing it for our Heavenly Father even more than for our husband.

My grandma assured us that the Lord will reward wives for responding the way He instructs in the Bible, for allowing their husbands to take the responsibility for the final call, trusting the Lord in the process. She pointed out that God loves us and will always make things ultimately turn for our good when we trust in Him and do things as He directs us.

She stressed that God never asks us to submit to decisions that contradict His Word, and therefore, cause us to do something immoral and violate our consciences. We must please God more than anyone else, even our husbands. But if our husbands' decisions are moral according to the Bible, we can yield knowing God will, in the big picture, work things out for us as we choose peace in our marriages and homes.

"Chances are our husbands won't make the perfect decision every time, despite our excellent advice and perspective," my grandma chuckled. "But we're not perfect either, and we have to be wives who are willing to let our men grow, so they can become the great leaders they were meant to be, one decision at a time."

Since women are great leaders, too, maybe that's why God is especially pleased when we don't insist on our own way all the time, running our homes by ourselves, undervaluing what our husbands' God-given roles and abilities are. Again, I was reminded of those verses in 1 Corinthians about true love that seeks others before self and sees the value in them, believing the best.

Listening to my grandma, I realized our leadership qualities as women aren't eliminated or negated by submission in marriage. Quite the opposite, we must be strong leaders to fulfill our call as women of God, wives, and mothers! Yet we use our gifts and talents for peace and success rather than a continual power play. And in *choosing* to rule ourselves and show respect, lies incredible power.

Cassie seemed to understand that power already. She had respected Brian for years by not showing how much she loved him before they were ready to date, by caring more for his dream to be an attorney (and what that would require) than her desire to have a boyfriend as a teenager. She also had dreams regarding her own career, ones she wanted to focus on and pursue without romance in the mix too early.

I was thrilled to be Cassie's maid of honor and felt privileged to be giving her a personal shower in just an hour. She and Brian were like family to me, and I loved them both very much.

Putting the finishing touches on the decorations, I looked around and thought, *In two short weeks, my dearest friend is going to be a married woman. If that hasn't hit her yet, it will when she opens the lingerie she's about to get!*

Brian's brother, James, was throwing a bachelor party for him at their parents' house. Both the bride and groom would be experiencing some unavoidable embarrassment and a lot of teasing in the next few hours, but that's tradition!

On the Terrace

Cassie, her mom, and her three sisters arrived at my house before the other shower guests. My mother took the flowers they had brought for the party and arranged them on the food table.

Cassie gave me a big hug when she saw how beautiful everything was. "This looks amazing, Julia!" Pulling me off to the side, she admitted, "I'm a little nervous."

"Tonight's a breeze," I replied, grinning. "Soon it will be your wedding night—then you'll have reason to be nervous!"

Cassie immediately jabbed me. "Save the kidding until I open my gifts. Just remember, one day it's going to be *your* turn."

One by one, the rest of the girls arrived. When Melody walked in, she gave me a genuine smile, the first in weeks. It felt good to be close to her again.

For the next three hours, we had a fabulous girls' night, laughing, talking, eating, and having tons of fun watching Cassie blush over all her gifts. But then, what were the guys doing and saying at their party? Although I knew they weren't doing anything bad, just playing video games and eating pizza, I still didn't want to know.

Cassie and I had made plans for her to sleep over after the shower. We knew this would be our last chance to be together as single friends.

Once the party had broken up and the guests had all gone, we helped my mom pick up the family room and kitchen. Then we put on our pajamas and stayed up most of the night, reminiscing. We had grown up sharing so much of our lives together; it was fun to relive it all. It was a special time we would always remember.

Before we knew it, two weeks had sped by, the rehearsal dinner had come and gone, and it was the day of Cassie's wedding. All the bridesmaids dressed at the church. Cassie was a vision in her gown. Every time we looked at each other, we had to fight back the tears. "Mascara!" we would laugh, waving our hands before our eyes to dry them. Vanity definitely has a way of helping you control your emotions.

The ceremony was underway promptly at three-thirty. As I walked down the center aisle, I caught a glimpse of the handsome Dr. Stanton sitting on the groom's side. My best friend was about to get married, and all I could think of at that moment was how amazing David looked. He smiled at me admiringly.

Smiling back, I turned my attention once again to the front of the church where I received a similar smile from Paul, who was standing in line with the other groomsmen, watching me intently.

I hope you already have your bags packed, I thought to myself, veering off to the left to join the other bridesmaids. After the little flower girl and ring bearer had successfully completed their assignments, the congregation stood at the pastor's request. Holding on to her father's arm at the back of the church, Cassie looked radiant. While she and her dad slowly made their way down the aisle, I turned to observe Brian's face as he adoringly watched his bride walking toward him. How happy he looked!

Once Cassie arrived at his side, my job of attending to her began: adjusting her train, holding her flowers, supplying her with a tissue when needed, and safely delivering Brian's wedding ring to her at the appropriate time.

The ceremony was beautiful. I had to bite my lip to keep from crying as Brian and Cassie took their vows. I loved them both, and witnessing their happiness was truly wonderful.

Fortunately, being the maid of honor, I couldn't give in to sentiment; I had work to do. After Brian kissed his bride, I handed Cassie her bouquet and straightened her train again. Then the newlyweds were introduced to the congregation for the first time as Mr. and Mrs. Brian Douglas. The recessional music began, and they led the way out of the sanctuary, with the rest of the wedding party following directly behind them. Lining up in the foyer, we greeted the guests. Then we posed for pictures.

Brian and Cassie hadn't rented a limousine because of the cost, but their parents pitched in together and surprised them with one. James and I rode in it with them to the reception, cruising downtown first to lengthen the ride.

It was six-thirty by the time we got to the country club. Most of the guests were already seated, waiting for the bride and groom to arrive. James made sure the DJ was ready before we lined up at the entrance to the dining room. As the wedding party and newlyweds were announced, we all marched in triumphantly, taking our assigned seats at the head table.

I had so much fun sitting next to Cassie on her special day. She was glowing, the happiest I'd ever seen her. Thrilled to be having such an elegant reception, she was having the time of her life.

The owner of the country club had certainly kept his word to my parents. The staff had gone all out to make the evening memorable in every way; the decorations, sparkling grape juice for the toast, food, service, and wedding cake were all outstanding.

After dinner, Brian and Cassie went around to all the tables, personally greeting their guests and thanking them for coming. I used the downtime to say hello to my family and then find David's table to talk to him for a few minutes.

"You look sensational, Julia," he said, rising to greet me. "I know you're in demand tonight, but save a dance for me, will you?"

"I was hoping you'd ask."

Our conversation was suddenly interrupted when Paul came up behind me, taking hold of my arm. "Come on, beautiful—they're ready to start the dancing."

I barely had time to excuse myself before he pulled me away. I felt like yanking away from him for being so rude, but I reminded myself that this was Brian and Cassie's special night. I wasn't about to spoil it. Putting on a smile, I took my place beside James, and we watched the bride and groom dance to the first song. Eventually, the wedding party joined in. I was glad to be dancing with James, grateful I wasn't paired up with Paul.

From the moment the music began, I did everything I could to avoid eye contact with Paul. I knew he wanted to dance with me, so I was deliberately staying as far away from him as I could, sticking close to Cassie when they cut the cake, steering clear of the dance floor. Without knowing it, Cassie's sister Amy was helping me out by keeping close to Paul. Since they were standing up together, he was expected to dance with her, and from all appearances, she had a crush on him.

You can have the guy, I thought. *Only I feel sorry for you if you ever want to break up with him!*

While Cassie was dancing, I noticed her bustle pulling loose. After I finished fixing it for her, I could see Paul in my peripheral vision, coming toward me. As he approached where I was standing, I heard David's voice directly behind me. "I believe this is our dance, Julia." Quickly, he whisked me away, right from under Paul's nose.

My hero had saved me once again from an unwanted admirer. How good it felt to be in his arms! In all the times we had been together, this was the first time we had been this close. He was a wonderful dancer, and we stayed together on the floor until it was time for Cassie to throw her bouquet. Then I had to leave David to join the rest of the single women who were already starting to assemble. After some serious scrambling, Melody caught the flowers. We all laughed at the coincidence since she was getting married next.

Immediately, the music resumed with a romantic favorite of mine, *The Way You Look Tonight*. Before I could locate David again, Paul whirled me around, and the next thing I knew, I was in his arms.

"At last!" he sighed, holding me close, making the most of the moment. "I've been trying to get a dance with you all night. David didn't seem to have much trouble, did he?"

I wanted to blurt out, "That's because I *want* to dance with him!" But I bit my tongue and remained silent.

Halfway through the song, Paul received a tap on the shoulder as someone matter-of-factly stated, "Cutting in." Thinking it was David, Paul turned abruptly, no doubt to refuse. When he saw it was my father, however, he immediately released me. "Of course," he said, noticeably disappointed.

My dad stepped in, and we glided to the other side of the dance floor. "This song was written for a girl like you, Julia," he reflected as we danced together. "The way you look tonight, I probably won't have this dance long, I fear."

"Thanks, Dad," I laughed. "Are you and Mom having fun?"

"Yes, but we're leaving after this song. Your grandparents are getting tired; we need to get them home. Your mother already has them in the car."

"I really appreciate all you did to make this such a special reception for Cassie and Brian."

"Thank the Lord, Julia. He made it all possible. And He isn't finished blessing the newlyweds. Calvin just showed me the final bill; he waived the gratuity charge. The kids don't owe the country club anything for tonight."

"That's amazing, Dad!" I replied just as the song ended. My father gave me a hug and escorted me off the floor, over to where David was standing, watching us dance.

"You don't have your car here, Julia," my dad reminded me once we reached David. "How are you getting home?"

"I'll be glad to bring her home, Mr. Duncan."

"Thanks, David. I appreciate it. Well, good night, you two. Have fun. Once I say goodbye to Brian and Cassie, I'm out of here."

After my dad walked away, David took my hand and led me out on the terrace. It was a balmy summer evening with a clear sky and thousands of stars twinkling overhead.

"May I have the pleasure of this next dance?" he asked, gathering me in his arms at my *yes*. When the music began, I recognized the tune immediately: *A Wink and a Smile.*

"I asked the DJ to play this song," he said, drawing me close. "It fits us, doesn't it?"

"Yes, I think it does," I sighed, contentedly. For the rest of the song, we were lost in the moment. The magic was interrupted when Amy found us and announced that Brian and Cassie had changed clothes and were leaving. We quickly found them to say goodbye.

"Pray for me," Cassie whispered in my ear.

"I will," I whispered back, knowing what she meant. A group of us lined up outside to throw confetti at them when they came out of the building. Once they were gone, we all went back inside. The DJ had already started packing up, and people began leaving.

Before I could gather my things, Paul walked up, stepping right between David and me. "I'll bring my car around, Julia, and take you home. We need to talk."

"Actually, I'm taking Julia home," David informed him.

"Listen," Paul said indignantly, "you've been monopolizing Julia all night. I barely had a chance to dance with her because of you. Now it's my turn to be with her."

David wasn't intimidated at all. He calmly looked at me. "Would you rather have Paul take you home?"

"No, thanks."

"There you are," David remarked with a winning grin. "It just doesn't seem to be your night, I guess."

Paul was furious at that remark and clinched his fist as though he were about to throw a punch. Without flinching, David stepped closer and stared him down.

"We're the ones who need to have a talk, Paul, to get a few things settled between us, but not here, not now. Just let it go and leave."

Angry but in control again, Paul simply glared at David and walked away.

"Sorry, Julia," David lamented, shaking his head. "Are you ready to go?" I nodded *yes* and walked over to the head table to get my purse.

Arriving at my house about twenty minutes later, I was sure David was going to kiss me for the first time. But wouldn't you know it, as we were standing on the doorstep, just when David began to lean down, the headlights from my parents' car shined on us as they turned into the driveway. My parents must have stayed at my grandparents' house for a while after taking them back home. I tried to hide my disappointment at their bad timing. My dad lowered his window and invited David in for a cup of coffee.

"Thanks anyway," he replied. "I have rounds early tomorrow morning before church. I should be going so I can get some sleep."

My dad nodded and then pulled into the garage. David looked back at me and smiled before saying good night. It wasn't a total loss because I did get kissed, sort of—one sweet peck on the cheek, not at all what I'd been hoping for earlier.

I passed my parents on the way upstairs to my room moments later. My dad apologized, "Hope we didn't interrupt anything just now, honey."

"I think you might have, actually."

"Was my girl about to be kissed?" my dad teased.

"We'll never know now, will we?" I responded good-naturedly over my shoulder as I continued up the staircase. I heard my parents laughing *good night* as I closed the door to my room.

I kept my promise and prayed for Cassie before falling asleep. That night I dreamed about David. When I awoke the next morning, I still hadn't managed to get kissed, not even in my dream.

Flight 459

I t's funny how adrenaline works. For weeks I'd been pumped, super charged with all I had to do for Cassie's wedding. Now that it was over, I felt like a balloon that had lost its air. All I wanted to do the next morning was stay in bed and *sleep in*. I couldn't remember the last time I'd done that. Where were the good old days when I could snooze until noon? Somewhere back in my high school years, I guess. But it was Sunday, and I needed to get up and start getting ready for church.

A refreshing shower helped to wake me up. Afterwards, I stood for the longest time in my closet, staring at my clothes, trying to make a selection. David had said I looked sensational the night before. Today he would have to settle for something a little less breathtaking.

I couldn't make up my mind between two dresses, so I took the scientific approach and tossed a coin. Tails won—the blue cotton print. Next, I had to find some nylons. The ones I had worn the night before had a slight run in them. In our family, pants weren't an option on Sunday mornings. It was a special request of my dad's. "I like to see my girls in skirts and dresses at church," he would always say.

My dad and brother had their own dress code as well: a suit or sport coat. Through the years, our tradition relaxed for the evening and mid-week services, but dressing up for Sunday mornings was expected. It wasn't for spiritual reasons or anything; it was just my dad's preference. But I was happy to oblige, knowing it meant something to him.

So far, David had worn a suit every Sunday morning since attending our church. Just one more reason for my dad to like him.

I was disappointed when church started and David wasn't there. It must have taken him longer than usual to complete his rounds because he didn't arrive until halfway through worship. At his request, the couple toward the end of the pew scooted over and made room for him next to me. Yep, he was wearing a suit again. Paul, meanwhile, was somewhere in the background, glaring at us. I'd become accustomed to it and had learned to ignore him.

It was beautiful outside that day, so after church David asked me if I would like to eat lunch at the park.

"Sure! How about I ride home with my parents while you go change and pick up Sandy? I can change, too, and pack a lunch for us by the time you come get me."

"You don't have to do that, Julia. We can buy something to take to the park."

"No, really, I'd like to make a picnic for us."

He seemed happy with the plan. I was, too, feeling confident I could at least make a delicious *sandwich*. There was a whole bowl of my mom's potato salad in the refrigerator, so once I added some melon, a few homemade cookies, and a thermos of lemonade, we'd have a great lunch to take.

An hour later, we were pulling into the parking lot at Murphy's Landing. Sandy was wagging her tail and licking David on the face, anxious to get out of the car. "Okay, okay, girl—calm down," he said, pushing her away. "You know the rules. You have to be on a lead until we get into the park." Sandy looked up at him expectantly, as if asking him to reconsider.

"Here, let me have her," I offered, attaching the leash to her collar.

"Thanks, I'll get the picnic basket out of the trunk."

As I stooped down outside the car to pet Sandy, she gave me a few wet kisses. Laughing, I spoke softly in her ear while David had his head inside the trunk. "Too bad your master isn't as free with his kisses as you are, girl."

"You say something?" David asked, slamming the trunk closed.

"Nope, just talking to Sandy," I answered coyly, straightening up. That's the wonderful thing about dogs. You can tell them all your secrets, knowing they will never be repeated.

When we reached a grassy section in the park, David took off Sandy's leash and let her run. As he watched her, I could tell she meant a lot to him, and I was thankful Sandy had accepted me into their world. David said she had never taken to anyone the way she had to me. They say dogs can sense things, so I wondered exactly what she was sensing. This was one time I wished she *could* talk.

David spread out the blanket, and then we unpacked our lunch. It was a perfect afternoon as we sat relaxing, talking, and laughing together. "I'm impressed, Miss Duncan," David said at one point, reaching for another sandwich. "Everything is delicious."

"Well, I can only take credit for the sandwiches. I made the bread in our bread machine earlier, but my mom made the potato salad and cookies. Oh, wait, I made the lemonade, too!" I laughed, watching David as he sampled the cookies next.

"You're both good cooks then. For this bachelor, homemade food is a special treat. I can't tell you how much I'm enjoying this, Julia." I was suddenly struck with how much I was enjoying making him happy.

After eating, we played with Sandy until it was time to clean up and go back home. I had some studying to do before the evening church service, and David still needed to prepare his lesson for his boys' group.

For the next few weeks, we saw each other briefly at the Center, but rarely on weekends, other than at church and at the park on Sunday afternoons. I was working on a paper that was due soon, and David was attending various Friday and Saturday night seminars with Dr. Feinberg.

Meanwhile, a couple from church, who also lived in our neighborhood, had just sold their home, not mentioning who had purchased it. I had asked my grandfather if he knew who was moving in there, but he just waved off my question and changed the subject. I wondered what that meant but didn't think about it again until we were all gathered for a Saturday-night family dinner.

Getting everyone's attention, my grandfather announced that he had some news for us. We were already excited because in one week my brother and his family were returning from Chile. We assumed they would stay with us until they decided where they wanted to relocate and could find a place of their own.

What we didn't know was John had emailed our grandfather six months earlier and asked him to look around for a house for them in Weston. When John found out that house in our neighborhood was selling, he told our grandfather to look no further. He'd played there many times as a boy and had always liked it.

With the discreet help of our grandfather, the deal was negotiated, agreed upon, and closed via phone, faxes, emails, and electronic funds transfers. Even my parents didn't know until that night. John wanted it to be a big surprise, but it could no longer be kept secret. Due to a mix-up with the dates, the furniture and belongings John and Jenny had in storage were being delivered a few days *before* their return from Chile. Grandpa suggested the whole family pitch in and work to get their house in move-in condition in time for their arrival.

At last, John and Jenny were coming home! It had been four long years since I had seen them. I'd never seen my niece, Magda, in person, and I was anxious for her to know her Aunt Julia better. My parents had flown out to visit them many times, but I was never able to go because of classes and my job at the Center.

My mother shed tears of joy when she found out they had decided to settle in Weston now that they were coming back to the States. She had promised herself not to get her hopes up. My grandfather explained that John had taken a new job as an engineer for a company whose office was only thirty minutes away. After being gone for so long, he and Jenny wanted to live close by family.

Later that night, I emailed John and Jenny to tell them we knew about the house and were counting the days until they'd be home for good. With only five days to get their new place cleaned and ready, my mom was on a mission! Everyone joined in to help; even Cassie and Brian found time to come over. David made my day by showing up one afternoon with pizza and soda for everyone.

By the day they were to arrive, John and Jenny's new home was ready. Of course, they would have to rearrange things how they wanted, but it was a good starting point at least. By noon, my parents, grandparents, and I were all standing in the airport at the baggage pick-up for Flight 459, watching intently for John, Jenny, and Magda.

My grandfather spotted them first. "There they are," he announced, pointing straight ahead.

We about smothered John and Jenny with all of us trying to hug and kiss them at the same time. Holding tight to her mother's hand, I'm sure little Magda didn't know what to think. Once we all settled down, John and my dad started looking for their baggage on the carousel. Meanwhile, Jenny introduced me to Magda.

I had spoken to Magda lots of times on Skype, of course, but I wondered how she would react to meeting me for real. I kneeled down and asked if Aunt Julia could give her a hug. Recognizing me, she gave me a big squeeze and kissed my cheek. I absolutely melted. I didn't feel like sharing her with my mom, but Grandma wanted a hug, too, as well as everybody else.

It wasn't until we got them all home that I had a chance to hold Magda again. What a sweet little girl! I was so happy John and Jenny had found her in an orphanage near where they had lived in Chile. I don't think John had ever thought about adopting a child before meeting Magda, but for Jenny it was a natural response since she'd been adopted herself. The first time they saw her, Jenny said she knew Magda was their little girl.

"So, Aunt Julia, what do you think of your niece?" my brother asked.

"She's adorable, John."

"Nice shirt she's wearing, huh?" he said, pointing to it.

I hadn't even noticed. She was sitting on my lap, so I turned her around to get a closer look. On the front of her shirt were the words BIG SISTER.

I quickly turned to John in surprise. "Are you serious?"

He looked at Jenny and laughed. "Yep, we're pregnant!" Now the hugs and kisses started all over again.

"When?" my mom wanted to know.

Jenny answered, "Six more months; sometime in February."

"Boy or girl?"

"Don't know, Mom," John replied. "We want to be surprised."

"Well, he or she, this baby will be loved," my dad said, clapping my brother on the shoulder in congratulations. "Let's eat and celebrate!"

My mother had asked Kitty to come over earlier and put out a nice dinner for us. It was ready and waiting, so we had a wonderful family meal together for the first time in four years.

Afterwards, I asked to be the one to give Magda her bath. My mom and I filled the tub with bubbles and gave her some cute bath toys we had gotten for her. We had fun watching her play, pinching ourselves that John and his family were really back. Once she was in her pajamas, we watched her kneel by her bed and say her prayers, first in English, then in Spanish. Too precious!

After Magda was in bed for the night, my grandparents left, but my parents and I stayed and talked with Jenny and John for a while. When my dad noticed John's eyes drooping, he got up and announced that we should go, too.

As John was walking us to the door, he turned to me and asked, "So when do we get to meet your doctor friend?"

"Tomorrow at church," I answered, calmly. Had John been a mind reader, he would have heard me secretly tack on, *"And I can't wait!"*

Chapter 12

The Letter

When I awoke on Sunday morning, I took a few minutes to lie in bed and think. Smiling to myself, I realized I had never been busier *or* happier. My heart was overflowing with peace concerning my past, thankfulness for my present, and high expectations for my future. As I lay there, I felt the arms of contentment embrace me, a feeling few other emotions can equal.

I knew some of my good feelings that morning had to do with my brother's return from South America with his family. But that wasn't the main reason. In Proverbs 13:12, the Bible says: "Hope deferred makes the heart sick, but when the desire comes, it is a tree of life." Waiting so long for my Mr. Right to appear had caused me to become heartsick at times, but being with David now was fulfilling my heart's desire. His friendship had become *a tree of life* for me, and I felt like I would burst with happiness at the thought of what might be.

I was excited to have John meet David at church that day; I so wanted them to like each other. As it turned out, they did, immediately. I could tell Jenny liked David, too. Even little Magda took to him. She insisted on climbing up in his lap during the sermon. Paul was sitting across the way where Cassie's sister Amy had scooted in next to him. She seemed annoyed that we were getting more of his attention than she was.

After the service, John spent some time catching up with Brian and Cassie. Then he and Jenny met Flip and Melody. Pastor Jack walked over to welcome John's family back to Weston Christian Center. "I look forward to seeing you guys get involved," he added once he knew they were staying in town permanently.

My mother had a big dinner planned, so our whole family was invited back to our house to eat, including David. He ran home, changed clothes, and took Sandy out first. Before he arrived, Jenny asked me, "Who was the guy staring at us in church?"

"That was Paul. He's jealous of David."

"That's obvious. I thought you stopped seeing him a long time ago."

"I did, but it's a case of *he won't give up* and *I won't give in*, a real stalemate."

"Are you and David officially dating?"

"Well, that's a good question. We see each other whenever we can, and it feels like more than friends... but he hasn't kissed me yet or anything."

"That's not a bad thing, Julia. Maybe God's keeping the brakes on things for a while for reasons you don't know now."

"Maybe. I only know I love being with him."

Our conversation was interrupted by David's arrival. A few minutes later, the family sat down for lunch together. Afterwards, we women moved into the kitchen to tackle the cleanup while the men went into the living room to watch sports, of course. Seeing the huge mess before us, I whispered to Jenny that somehow the tradition of the women cleaning while the men relaxed could not have been divinely inspired! She laughed her agreement.

When the last pot was dried and put away, we joined the men. John and David were sitting on the floor building a tower with Magda. Or should I say, Magda was watching them build *their* tower. It looked far too advanced for a four-year-old.

David noticed Magda was getting bored, so he shoved the rest of the blocks over toward John and went into the foyer where he had set his bag. Reaching inside, he pulled out a stethoscope and brought it back with him. "Would you like to hear something special, Magda?"

She looked up at him wide-eyed and nodded. David showed her how to insert the earpieces. "Now listen," he instructed her, holding the other end of the instrument against his chest. "That thumping is my heart beating."

"Corazón," Madga responded.

"That's right, honey—heart."

"Do you speak Spanish?" my grandfather asked from the recliner in the corner of the room.

"I know enough to get by. For a doctor, it can be helpful with so many Spanish-speaking people in our country."

I had just learned two things about David I hadn't known before: he could speak Spanish and was wonderful with children. The fact that he was bilingual impressed me, but his rapport with Magda trumped that.

The following week I was flying high, happy my whole family liked David, that he got along so well with them. Things were great with us, too. We played racquetball and met for lunch twice. My extra free time was rapidly coming to an end, however; fall classes were starting up again on Monday.

I was looking forward to spending Sunday with David after church. He had mentioned at racquetball that we might go for a drive after lunch. To my delight, the weather was perfect, and I felt especially pleased with the way I looked that morning—good hair days are the best!

All my enthusiasm dwindled, however, when I didn't see David at church. "He must have been called to the hospital," I reasoned, quite disappointed. Then, when I was talking to Cassie after service, I saw him out of the corner of my eye in the back of the sanctuary. Giving Cassie a quick hug goodbye, I happily made my way through the crowd to where he was standing. From the moment we greeted each other, I could tell something was wrong. He was acting funny.

"Are you okay?" I asked, concerned.

"Sure, I'm fine," he responded without much emotion. "I was up late last night. I'm tired, I guess. In fact, I think I'll go home, grab something to eat, and sleep for a while this afternoon."

"Okay, are you coming tonight?"

"No, Jeremy's leading my group for me." Seeming anxious to leave, he didn't elaborate. "See you later," he offered as a token farewell. Then he walked away, not once looking back.

I stood there dumbfounded, unable to comprehend what had just happened. I didn't have time to think it through because by now my parents had caught up with me.

"I saw you talking to David," my mom said. "Are you leaving with him or coming with us?"

"I'm coming with you guys," I replied, trying to act normally. I was glad we didn't go out to eat that day. I wanted to go home and try to make sense of the way David was acting. Sitting in the back seat on the drive home, I mentally analyzed the last time he and I had been together—Friday for lunch. Everything was fine then. We had fun talking and laughing, and when David walked me to my car, for a split second, I felt he was resisting the impulse to kiss me goodbye.

Suddenly, a thought flashed through my mind when we pulled into the garage. While my parents were busy in the kitchen getting lunch ready, I ran up to my room. Paul had sent me an email earlier in the week. I'd passed it off at the time as another one of his attempts to discredit David. I had sent a short reply before deleting it, so that meant I still had a copy of Paul's email in my sent folder. I pulled it up to read it again:

> *Julia,*
> *You've known me a lot longer than David Stanton. Trust me, this guy's a fake. You're not the only woman he's chasing after. When I came out of the bathroom Sunday night, Stanton was in the hallway talking on his cell. I overheard his conversation with some Cynthia, and the way he was talking, there's no way she's just a friend. Before he hung up, he said he couldn't wait to see her when he came home.*
>
> *Wise up, Julia, before you get hurt.*
>
> *Paul*

My reply to him read:

> *You overheard or you eavesdropped? After the way you've been lately, what makes you think I'd believe this? Give it up, Paul. It's time for you to go home and get on with your life!*

Reading his email again, fear struck my heart. What if Paul was right? What if David did have a romance going on that I knew nothing about? Could this be the reason he had never kissed me in all the months we'd been seeing each other? Was friendship all he wanted from our relationship? Did he sense I wanted more and was now backing off?

Immediately, I scolded myself for thinking such things. The last time I had failed to research the facts, jumping to conclusions about David, my rival turned out to be a *dog!* I'd promised myself then to always give David the benefit of the doubt. Here was my chance.

If Paul *had* overheard David talking to a girl, which I didn't even know was true, this Cynthia could be anyone, maybe even a relative. Who knows what was said? It could have been anything, quite innocent despite Paul's obsession to hear the worst.

Determined to think the best, I deleted Paul's email permanently and consoled myself that David must not have been feeling well. That's why he acted the way he did at church. Relieved, I slipped into some jeans and a top and went downstairs to help with lunch.

While we were eating, my dad asked if David was coming over. "Not today, Dad. I think he's fighting a cold or something."

I expected David to rest all afternoon, but I was hoping I'd hear from him after I got home from church that night. Much to my disappointment, he didn't call or try to contact me until Tuesday when I received a short, impersonal email saying that something came up and he had to cancel our racquetball dates for the next two Wednesdays.

What is this? I thought, fighting tears. *Why the sudden change toward me?* My pride wouldn't allow me to call him. That would've been too much like running after him. But when I hadn't heard from David by the next Sunday morning, I made up my mind to corner him and find out what was going on. We'd been spending time together since April, and I felt I had the right to some answers. If he didn't want to see me anymore outside of church, he could at least have the courtesy to come out and say so.

I never got the chance to confront him at church that morning because he wasn't there. I found Pastor Kevin and asked if he'd seen David. "He's out of town until Saturday, Julia, visiting his family, I think. He got Jeremy to cover for him while he's gone, but he'll be back again next week." He seemed surprised I didn't know. No more surprised than I was.

My first impulse was to call David on his cell as soon as I got home, but then I decided that wouldn't be wise. I was angry and didn't want to say something I might regret later. I needed to cool down and wait until Saturday when I could talk to him face to face.

You don't hide anything from my mom very long. She had noticed I hadn't mentioned David in a week but didn't want to pry. Seeing how upset I appeared after church, she asked if I needed to talk when we got home. I explained to her how David had suddenly stopped communicating with me.

"I don't know why the sudden change, Julia," she said, putting her arm around me. "But I do know David really cares about you. He's proven that in many ways. I'm sensing in my spirit that you're in the middle of a big misunderstanding. I'm sure when he gets back, you'll get things all straightened out."

I'd learned to trust my mom's instincts. Maybe she was right. I just couldn't figure out what could have caused any misunderstanding between David and me. From my point of view, things were going great until this happened. I kept hoping he would call me before Saturday, but he didn't.

Because I had no way of knowing what time David would actually be getting back, I made sure all my studying was done for the weekend by noon on Saturday. After lunch, I helped my parents rake leaves for a couple of hours to kill some time. Then I went upstairs to read my Bible and pray.

When I got to my room, I pulled out my cell phone and placed it on the desk. Then I sat down and stared at it as though I could make it ring just by wishing. If I hadn't heard from David by six o'clock, my plan was to call him. I was already starting to get nervous. I desperately wanted to talk to him, but I was also afraid of what he might say—afraid that something had happened to change the way he felt about me. Needing comfort, I opened my Bible and read several passages. Then I reached for my journal and began writing a prayer:

Heavenly Father, I'm really scared. I've been careful not to admit it to anyone, not even myself, but I love David. I don't want to lose him. I can't imagine loving anyone else as much as him. Just when my hopes were soaring, this happened. But what did happen? I have to know.

When I call David, please let me reach him right away. I want to talk to him before I see him at church tomorrow, assuming he's even there. Seeing him without talking to him first would be so awkward. If he was as cold to me as the last time I saw him, I think I'd burst into tears on the spot. I can't bear to think that things might never be the same between us again, that I'll have to start all over believing for the right man. Forgive me; I'm imagining the worst. Yet despite all my fears, there is still a calm I can't explain. It's almost as though You're saying, "All is well, Julia. Continue to trust Me."

Before I could write any more, my mother came into my room and handed me a letter. "This came in the mail for you, Julia. I'm going to take a short nap before starting dinner, so grab the phone if it rings, will you? Dad's out running a few errands."

"Sure thing, Mom."

Once she left for her room, I examined the envelope. It didn't have a return address on it, just my name and address on the front. Curious to see what was inside, I reached for my opener and slit the top.

Emptying the contents, I held a typed letter and a separate, sealed envelope with the words **READ THIS LAST** printed on the front. Immediately, I scanned to the end of this mysterious letter to see who had sent it.

"Not today," I muttered when I saw it was from Paul. What could he be up to now? Going back to the beginning, I started reading.

Julia,
By the time you read this, I will be halfway to the West Coast. I'm finally going home. I hadn't planned on saying anything to you; I was just going to disappear. But I had a last-minute change of heart. I am a Christian, even though I haven't been thinking and acting much like one lately.

Where do I begin? Maybe I should start with two Sunday nights ago. That was the same day your brother's family was in church for the first time after coming back. I never got to meet them, but they look like nice people.

Anyway, after the youth meeting that night, you said you had a headache and went home right away. David walked you to your car, remember? After you drove off, I caught up with him. It was my chance to finally confront him. I challenged David to a fight, but he refused. I HATE to admit it, but what he said made sense.

He asked what fighting would prove, saying that beating each other up wouldn't affect the way you feel about either of us. But he let me know that if I ever hurt you, he'd come after me; protecting you was something he was more than willing to fight for.

He said that as long as we were both in love with you, we'd never be friends. But we were brothers in Christ and needed to remember that people were watching how we treated each other. He said we were mentoring boys here at church and that the tension between us was setting a bad example for them.

He told me my problem was that I saw him as a wall between you and me, but you had put up that wall long before he came to Weston.

He went on to say it was your decision who you wanted to be with, not ours, that we needed to let you choose. He said you may not want him, either, and he'd have to live with his own disappointment. But until you told him no, he had a green light.

Funny he should use that example. You stopped going out with me because you said you saw a red light, and now he was taking you away from me because he was seeing a green light.

After talking to David, I was finally ready to give up. You called it right, Julia; you were the only reason I hung around in Weston after graduation. Knowing for sure I had no chance with you anymore, there wasn't any point in my staying here. I gave my two weeks notice at Lyndall's the next day.

I was angry and bitter about losing you, Julia. The last few years seemed like such a waste. If I couldn't have you, I didn't want David to, either. That's why I sent that last email to you. I had overheard David's call that Sunday night when he was talking to someone named Cynthia, but he never said anything romantic to her. That was a lie. I was just looking for a way to plant doubt in your mind about him. I figured it was my last chance to mess things up between you and David before I left town.

Little did I know, another chance was coming my way that Friday. I was in my office sorting through the invoices from the shop when I saw David was sending you flowers, requesting they be delivered on Saturday morning, no later.

I went out into the shop, and while our floral arranger was distracted with a customer, I pulled her order copy for your flowers. Attached to it was a sealed envelope that was to be inserted into the box with the flowers before delivery. Only now there wouldn't be a delivery; I'd make sure of that.

You probably noticed the enclosed envelope has been opened and resealed. Yes, I read it when I got home that night. At first I congratulated myself for sabotaging David's plans, happy that he'd feel some of the pain I did, but by the next morning, my conscience was really bothering me. I wanted to throw his message to you away, but I couldn't do it. Not because of David; I don't even like him. It was because of you, Julia. I realized if you really cared for him, I had no right to hurt you this way. I couldn't face you with what I'd done, so I made sure this letter would arrive after I'd already gone.

There's no good excuse for the way I've acted. I wanted you, I lost you, and I hate losing. David really is the better man; maybe that's why I dislike him so much. He told me the night of our show-down that you were a priceless treasure and not some cheap trophy we were fighting to win. He was right; you are a treasure. I'm not sure what I am right now, certainly not deserving of you. I hope one day you can forgive me.
Paul

I was so shocked and angry with Paul, I didn't want to deal with my feelings about him at the moment. All I cared about was opening the other envelope and reading David's message.

Julia,
I'm sending red roses this time to tell you I want to be much more than friends. If you feel the same way, meet me at Celestial Gardens tonight at eight. Be honest, Julia. Please don't come just to spare my feelings.
David

Tears in my eyes, I held the note close. Poor David! How hurt he must have been when I never showed up that Saturday! No wonder he was so cool toward me the next day at church. He was dealing with a ton of rejection while I acted like nothing was different between us. I didn't even mention getting his roses!

I wanted so much to make it all up to him, but how? Then I got an idea. Reaching for my phone, I called David's cell. He picked up on the third ring. He actually sounded happy to hear from me.

"Thanks for calling, Julia. I was driving along thinking about how much I missed talking to you."

"Me, too," I replied. "David, will you please give me a second chance?"

"What do you mean?"

"Meet me at Celestial Gardens at eight tonight."

"Is that what you really want?"

"Trust me—I've never been more sure of anything."

"Well, okay. I'm two hours out of Weston, so I can be at the restaurant by eight."

"Please hurry, David. I can't wait to see you!"

"Wow!" he exclaimed, pleased. "Just don't blame me if I get a speeding ticket."

A smile in my voice, I replied, "Get here safely, that's all I ask." Then we hung up.

My desire to strangle Paul was on hold. I was too happy about seeing David again. Fortunately for my mother, she wasn't asleep yet when I flew into her bedroom, unable to contain my excitement.

"I take it you've heard from David," she laughed, guessing the reason for my exuberance. I went over to her bed where we sat for the next few minutes as I told her about the letter, David's undelivered invitation, and my plans to meet him at Celestial Gardens at eight.

Shaking her head, she confessed, "I'm really disappointed in Paul. I never would've expected him to do something like this!"

"You said there had to be some kind of misunderstanding, Mom. Now we know what it was."

"But David still doesn't know what happened, right?"

"He will tonight!"

"Do you want me to drop you off at the restaurant? Something tells me you'll want David to drive you home."

I gave my mother a big hug. "Thank you! You're the best! Okay, I'd better go get ready. I have less than two hours to become irresistible!"

Chapter 13

A First

Before getting into the shower, I called the restaurant and tried to reserve a table. "Sorry, we don't take reservations on Saturday nights," the hostess informed me. I sounded so disappointed, she offered another solution. "What time will you be arriving?"

"Eight o'clock."

"All right, I'll put your name on the waiting list around seven-fifteen. That way a table should be available for you by eight, maybe sooner. You might want to get here a few minutes early."

Thanking her several times, I hung up and looked at the clock. It was going to take a miracle to get my hair washed, dried, and styled the way I wanted it on time, but I believed in miracles! Plugging in my curling iron before my shower and a little extra towel drying afterward did the trick.

When my hair was done, I grabbed my makeup bag and smoothed on my moisturizer and foundation. Planning for a dimly lit dining room, I selected a shimmering eye shadow. Then I tastefully lined my eyes, applied my long lash mascara, and brushed on just enough blush.

"Which shade of lipstick?" I pondered, sorting through several tubes. "*Kissable Pink* sounds promising," I smiled, setting it aside until I was fully dressed.

I already knew what I was wearing, saving me some time. I had recently bought a stunning black dress for just such an occasion. Zipping up the back, I stepped in front of my full-length mirror to look at my reflection. I knew this dress was for me the moment I saw it hanging on the rack. Made from a soft fabric with a fitted bodice and belted waist, its skirt flared out ever so slightly when I turned, gracefully settling in just above my knees. Absolutely perfect!

Trying to hurry, I quickly changed purses, making sure to insert Paul's letter and David's card inside. Reaching for my favorite perfume, I sprayed on a little and then slipped into my shoes.

"Oh, no," I cried, looking down at my hands. In all the excitement, I'd forgotten to put a fresh coat of polish on my nails. I didn't want to chance doing it myself now that I was dressed. Just then my mom came in to check on me and saved the day. Thanks to her, ten minutes later I had a new manicure.

"I'll meet you at the car, Julia. Better hurry; it's already seven-thirty," she announced before leaving.

"Be there in a minute," I called after her. I took one last look in the mirror. *Oops!* I'd almost forgotten the final touch—lipstick. *Kissable Pink* was still lying on my dressing table where I'd left it.

"Try and live up to your name tonight," I requested, applying it to my lips, taking care not to smudge my nails. Then I dropped the tube into my purse and snapped the purse shut.

My dad was standing in the foyer watching for me when I came downstairs. "I was waiting to see the finished product," he informed me, smiling. "You look lovely, sweetheart. Something tells me David won't be concentrating on the food tonight."

I couldn't help laughing. "That's the whole idea, Dad. Would you get my black cardigan out of the guest closet and drape it over my arm, please?"

When he returned with it, I warned him, "Please watch the nails! They're not quite dry yet."

My dad knew the drill. I often left for church with wet nails. He graciously walked me out to the car, opened the passenger door, and closed it once I was inside. Then my mom reached over to help me with my seat belt. Waving goodbye to my dad as we pulled out of the driveway, we headed for Celestial Gardens.

With good traffic on our side, I was at the restaurant by seven-fifty. The hostess informed me our table was next, so I took a seat on a bench to wait. Minutes later, just as she called out my name, David walked in. His eyes never left mine from the second he came through the door. Smiling as only David could, he leaned down and kissed me on the cheek.

"That's some dress," he whispered. "You look beautiful."

"Follow me, please," the hostess requested.

She seated us in a secluded little booth next to a window overlooking a lighted outdoor garden. Since it was a warm, fall evening, many couples were dining alfresco, but I was happy to be inside. Once we ordered our beverages, David reached for my hand across the table. "I'm so glad you called and asked to meet me here."

"Am I forgiven for not showing up two weeks ago?" I replied, smiling at him, bursting to tell him the truth.

He gently squeezed my hand. "Of course, Julia. I don't even want to know why it didn't work out before. All that matters is we're here together now."

I couldn't hold back any longer. "No, I want to tell you why I wasn't here that Saturday." Opening my purse, I removed his card and Paul's letter and slid them both over to him. "I never received your roses or this card, David. I knew nothing of them until the mail came today. I wasn't here that night because I never got the invitation."

David looked at me in disbelief. "I don't understand. How could that happen?"

"You'll understand once you read this letter."

I sat watching his reactions page by page. "What a jerk," he eventually muttered, clearly upset. Pointing to a passage in the letter, he said, "I'll give Paul credit for one thing. He was smart enough to leave town before I found out about this."

"I guess we have to be grateful he decided to tell me what he'd done."

"I know what you're saying, Julia, but right now I'm not feeling grateful to him for anything. It was only a matter of time before we would've found out on our own. But it might have taken longer, that much is true."

We had to stop talking to order. Actually, neither of us was there to eat, so we decided on a few appetizers.

"How long did you wait here for me to show up, David?"

"Oh, I don't know. Long enough to know you weren't coming. I deliberately set up our meeting the way I did to give you an easy out if you wanted one. Then when you didn't show up, I wasn't prepared for how hard it was going to hit me. I kept trying to convince myself that something must've gone wrong.

"When I got home, I pulled up my credit card account on my computer. Sure enough, the charge for your flowers was right there on the screen, so I felt sure they had been delivered. I barely slept that night trying to figure out how I could've so misread your feelings for me.

"I didn't want to go to church in the morning, but I figured I would have to face you sooner or later. It wasn't going to be easy anytime. Before I walked out the door, I got a call from my dad, asking if I could take some time off. My mother had gotten sick, and he felt she needed me to come home for a while. I called Dr. Feinberg right away. He said he'd been working me pretty hard and to take all the time I needed, that he'd get the other doctors to cover for me in the office and at the hospital.

"When I finally got to church, worship had already started. Pastor Kevin was walking into the sanctuary at the same time, so I asked him to get someone to take my group for that night as well as the following Sunday. I sat in the back for the rest of the service."

"Then I came along afterward, happy as could be, expecting things to be like usual. I can't imagine what you thought of me!"

"I have to admit that threw me, Julia. I expected you to be at least a little uncomfortable seeing me after standing me up. Nothing was making sense. It was like being in a bad dream. While we were talking in the back of the church, my insides were tied up in knots. The way you were acting was adding insult to injury. I was so hurt, I couldn't just stand there and exchange small talk with you. Being up most of the night, I knew I had to sleep for a while before getting on the road to Baymont. I used being tired as an excuse to get away from you as fast as I could and went back to my condo."

We paused again when our food arrived. Once the waitress was gone, I picked up where we had left off. "When you walked away from me so abruptly, I was stunned by how indifferent you were toward me. I couldn't come up with any reason for it, so I figured you weren't feeling well. I knew something else was wrong when you cancelled our racquetball dates in that short email you sent me. Plus, you weren't calling anymore. I didn't even know you were out of town until I asked Pastor Kevin about you last Sunday."

"I didn't call you for a couple of reasons, Julia. For one thing, I wasn't sure what you wanted from our relationship. I certainly didn't want to push myself on you if you weren't interested in going forward. You'd had enough of that with Paul. At the same time, I didn't want to continue as we were.

"Another reason had to do with how busy I was handling family problems. Since my sister died, my mother's been on a lot of different medications. My dad called because she'd had a serious reaction from combining drugs. We found out she had more than one doctor prescribing for her. By the time I got home, our family physician had put her in the hospital for observation. My dad felt my being home would be the best medicine for her. While there, I researched everything she was taking and put together a program to help her slowly wean herself off her prescriptions and replace them with natural alternatives. I doubt she'll follow my advice, but at least I tried."

Gesturing toward Paul's letter again, David explained, "Just to set the record straight, Cynthia was my sister's best friend. They were very close, a lot like you and Cassie. She's like another sister to me. My mother has become very attached to her since Carrie's death. In an unhealthy way, I think she still feels a connection to Carrie when Cynthia is around, even though she's nothing like my sister."

By now we had finished eating our appetizers. Sitting back in my chair, I reflected, "We were both miserable for almost two weeks. Paul definitely messed things up, didn't he?"

"He did, but as wonderful as you look tonight, I'm done talking about him. Let's get out of here."

I was just as ready as he was. After paying the check, he asked me where I had parked my car. When I told him my mom had brought me so I could ride home with him, his face lit up. "I knew I liked that woman," he said with a wink.

Twenty minutes later, we were holding hands, walking down the pier at Murphy's Landing, slowly making our way toward the empty observation gazebo. There was a slight breeze that night, but the air was comfortably warm. The moon, almost full, cast its glowing reflection on the water.

We stood there for a brief time side by side, watching the flickering lights along the far shoreline. Then David gently turned me toward him, took me in his arms, and smiled at me. He seemed to be studying my face, taking his time before he spoke. Finally, looking into my eyes, he said the words I had been longing to hear. "I love you, Julia, so very much."

"I love you, too, David—with all my heart."

Unable to hold back another second, he leaned down and pressed his lips against mine. Time seemed to stand still as we shared true love's first kiss, thrilling but tender.

When our lips parted, he held me close, and I heard him whisper, "Thank You, Lord." He didn't know it, but I was thanking God, too. Pulling back slightly, he reached into his coat pocket and pulled out a small, white box. "I have something for you to commemorate our first kiss." Surprised, I took it from his hand.

"You almost got this the night of Brian and Cassie's wedding," he said as I untied the satin bow. "But if you remember, we got interrupted before I could kiss you."

By now, I had removed the lid. My eyes grew wide when I saw what was inside—a stunning platinum chain with a diamond pendant heart, the word *first* engraved delicately on the back. "It's beautiful, David. I love it! Will you put it on for me?"

Carefully fastening the clasp, he then straightened the chain. "There," he said, admiring the pendant.

"How does it look?"

"Gorgeous, just like you. I had it made a while ago, you know. It just had a hard time finding its way around that pretty neck of yours. When I couldn't give it to you the night of the wedding, I moved to plan B two weeks ago. Thanks to Paul, you didn't show up that Saturday night, and it looked like I might *never* be able to give it to you. It's been hanging on the rear-view mirror of my car ever since. Each time I saw it, I'd pray, *If Julia and I are meant to be together, Lord, please help us to work things out.* And He did."

"I heard you thank Him after you kissed me tonight. I was thanking Him, too."

David pulled me close and kissed me again. Then we took a minute to pray and thank God together.

When we were done, David noticed the temperature was dropping and suggested we leave. The wind began whipping around us on our walk back up the long pier, so we doubled the pace hand in hand until we reached his car.

The ride back home was surreal as I held David's hand and thought about our evening together. The man of my dreams had just told me he loved me! Could this really be happening? How differently I had felt just hours ago!

All too soon, we were pulling into my driveway, and it was time to say goodbye. Neither of us wanted this night to end, but it was getting late, and there was always tomorrow to look forward to together. David walked me to the front door. As we stood there talking, I touched my necklace and thanked him again.

"I'm glad you like it," he said, taking both of my hands. "We experienced a first tonight, Julia. But this is just the start for us; we'll be having a lot of firsts together from now on. Tonight has been so perfect. I only have one regret."

"Really? What?"

"I'm sorry Paul wrote about my saying I was in love with you. You read that before I had a chance to tell you myself."

"Don't let that bother you. He may have written it in a letter, but I like the way you showed me tonight much better."

Breaking out in a grin, David said, "Really? Shall I show you again?"

"Please do," I requested, putting my arms around his neck. Then he kissed me once more before saying good night.

Stepping inside the house, I remained at the door and peeked out the sidelight to watch David walk to his car. As he drove away, I exhaled a contented sigh and turned to see that the downstairs was dark.

My mom had left a light on for me in the upper landing. I went upstairs, hoping my parents would still be awake. I wanted to share my fabulous evening with them. No light under their bedroom door meant they were already asleep; my news would have to wait until morning. I wasn't tired, but I decided to turn in for the night anyway, knowing I had to get up early for church.

Heading to my closet, I slipped out of my shoes and dress, putting them back in their places. I quickly got ready for bed, but before turning in, I found my evening purse, took out Paul's letter and David's card, and placed them both in my keepsake box on the corner of my desk. I sensed in my heart that David *was* my Mr. Right, the man God had chosen for me, but only time would tell for sure.

The suitor vase that my grandmother had given me was standing empty on my desk. "Sorry you missed out on David's roses," I softly lamented. I couldn't help but feel a little sad about that, but I had received what was more important: the card and declared love of the sender.

Squirming under the covers, I noticed I still had my necklace on. I carefully removed it, placed it on my night table, and turned out the light. Lying there in the dark, I thanked God again for all that had happened, reliving every beautiful moment in my mind's eye.

"So this is love," I whispered happily before drifting off into a blissful sleep.

The Real Thing

When my alarm went off the next morning, I jumped out of bed and ran downstairs to tell my parents about my special date with David. I found them in the kitchen, eating breakfast together. When I shared my big news, my mom and dad were pleased but certainly not surprised. As it turned out, they had a little confession to make: David had taken my father out to lunch weeks before to ask his permission to court me.

"When a man asks to court your daughter," my dad explained, "he's not asking you if he can call her up for a date now and then. Instead, he's telling you he wants to spend time with her because he has marriage in mind."

My mom added, "That's why I knew there had to be some kind of misunderstanding going on when you told me David suddenly changed the way he was acting toward you."

"Right," my dad inserted. "David's not the kind of man who says something one day, only to change his mind the next. He's too solid for that. He and I had a long talk that afternoon, Julia. All of us knew David had been a committed Christian for years, but there were some other things I wanted to know before giving him my consent to court you. Do you remember my story about what Grandpa Carl put me through before he would allow me to court your mother?"

"Yes, Dad, I love that story."

"I learned from your grandpa that when a father sees that someone is attracted to his daughter, he should take time to evaluate the man's character and intentions before his daughter falls in love with him. If you wait too long, the horse is already out of the barn, as they say, and it's often too late to get her to listen to reason if you think the man isn't right for her.

"Maybe you didn't know it, Julia, but I've been closely watching your friendship with David. I'm not sure exactly when I sensed he was in love with you; I think it was at Cassie's wedding. But if David hadn't arranged a time to talk to me, I would've called him myself. Not that I had any real concerns about him. You can tell a lot about a man by the way he handles himself. I'd had a chance to observe David during some stressful times, first with McNulty and then with Paul. I respect him greatly. He'd also passed the acid test with me: he looks me in the eye whenever I talk to him."

"I know how important that is to you, Dad."

"It is. I can remember when I couldn't look any man in the eye. That's why your grandpa put my relationship with your mother on hold until he could help me work through the rejection I had suffered because of my father. In my talk with David, I learned he has a great relationship with his dad. His mother is my only immediate concern.

"The loss of a child is no doubt one of the most devastating things a parent can experience, but it's been five years, Julia, and from what David's told me, she is still grief-stricken. Her inability to deal with her daughter's death is causing a lot of ongoing heartache in that family. Your mother and I have been praying for her ever since David shared that with me.

"As your father, I need to point out now that if you and David were to get married someday, you'd have to deal with Mrs. Stanton's emotional issues, too. I can't make that choice for you. I'm just saying it would be wise for you to spend some time with David's family *before* you commit to anything more."

I knew my father was right, but as he said, *the horse was already out of the barn*. I was in love with David, deeply in love, and I had faith that together we could face anything. I figured Mrs. Stanton's condition had a lot to do with all the prescriptions she was taking. I hadn't even met the woman yet. If David and I *did* get engaged, maybe the idea of having a daughter again would bring comfort to her troubled heart.

But this was no time to ponder problems. It was getting late, and I needed to get ready for church. David was picking me up so we could ride together. For now, life was wonderful. I was deliriously happy. The only thing causing me frustration was deciding what to wear.

Hurriedly, I showered, picked out an outfit, and dressed in time to greet David at the front door when he arrived. Seeing I was wearing my necklace, he gave me a sweet peck on the lips. *That'll do for now,* I thought.

My parents weren't quite ready, so we left ahead of them. While we were driving, David reached for my hand. "Julia, I've had time to think about Paul since last night."

"Me, too. Can you believe he actually charged your account for those flowers?"

"Oh, I'd forgotten that. I guess he wanted to keep us apart as long as he could. He probably figured I'd check online when you didn't show up. I don't mind paying that bill, though; it was a small price to pay to finally get rid of him. What I wanted to say was that even though we're both still angry at what he did, we need to forgive him and ask God to forgive him, too. If we wait until we feel like it, we might never do it."

I agreed. Once we reached the parking lot at church, we each prayed for Paul. It felt good to let my anger go. Although he'd been forgiven, neither of us would miss having him around. It was going to be wonderful to be together without having to deal with Paul's stares and sarcasm.

When we walked into the sanctuary that day, holding hands, the new status of our relationship was apparent to all. My brother smirked and then gave me a subtle little wink before greeting me with a hug. Smiles were coming our way from every direction in the congregation. Obviously, David and I hadn't been as good at concealing our feelings as we had thought. Now that we were openly expressing them, our family and friends were happy for us.

We sat next to my grandparents, making room for my mom and dad when they arrived. Cassie and Brian sat in the pew behind us beside John and his family. Once worship started, Cassie leaned forward and excitedly whispered in my ear, "Call me later. We need to talk!"

Smiling over my shoulder, I nodded that I would. After church, a whole group of us went to Benny's for lunch. Cassie and Brian already had plans with their parents and weren't able to join us. Afterwards, David dropped me off at my house so he could go home, unpack, and get some rest before the evening service. I was sleepy, too. As soon as I changed my clothes, I took a nap for a couple of hours. When I awoke, I called Cassie right away.

Much to my surprise, she already knew Paul had left town. He'd met Brian early Thursday morning for breakfast to say goodbye, and the whole story of my undelivered roses had come out in their conversation.

Cassie explained, "When Brian found out what Paul did to you, he was furious. He told Paul, 'This obsession you have for Julia has turned you into someone I don't even know! It's definitely time for you to go home, but before you do, you need to tell Julia the truth. You owe her that much.'

"Paul did feel bad about what he'd done. I think that's why he confessed it all to Brian; his conscience was really bothering him by then. Even so, he said he couldn't face you, that he'd send you a letter explaining everything. Since Brian had heard David was coming back home on Saturday, he made Paul promise to get it in the mail before leaving Weston. He wanted you to have the letter by the time David returned so the two of you could get everything straightened out. When Brian and I saw you and David walk into church holding hands, we figured Paul had kept his word. Still, Brian wanted me to talk to you this afternoon to make sure."

"Thanks, Cass. I'm glad you didn't say anything about this at church. David has forgiven Paul, but he'd also like to forget about him."

"Can't say I blame him. So, best friend, are you finally in love?"

"YES! For years I've watched this happen for others; finally it's my turn!"

"I'm *so happy* for you, Julia. David is such an amazing guy; Brian and I like him a lot. You two make a great couple. We've been wondering when you were going to admit your feelings for each other. But I guess Brian and I can't talk. Look how long it took us!"

"Oh, Cassie, I love David so much. I used to watch you and Brian together and wonder what it would be like to love and be loved that way. Now I know."

"When it's the real thing, it's worth the wait, isn't it?"

"Absolutely. It's like all the pain and frustration of waiting vanished the moment he said he loved me."

"Were you wearing a new necklace today?"

"David had it made for me to remember our first kiss."

"Oh, I still love to think of mine with Brian."

Once we finished chatting, I told Cassie I needed to call Jenny to fill her in on the new developments with David. Before hanging up, she reminded me, "When we break into our small groups tonight at church, the leaders are going read the story you and I wrote for the girls."

"Oh, that's right. We should make copies so the girls can each take one home afterwards."

"Good idea. I'll print off a bunch before church. See you then."

Cassie was referring to a cute story we wrote together about proper dress standards for Christian girls. Pastor Kevin had asked us to come up with an idea to show the girls in the youth group how the thought life of guys is affected by the way girls dress. Too many of our young women were wearing current fashions that left little to the imagination, exposing way too much skin.

I got part of the material for our story from a conversation I'd had with my grandparents during a family dinner one Sunday after church. Our youth group had given a special presentation that morning, and my grandfather was appalled by the way many of the girls were dressed.

"At the rate hemlines are going up and necklines are going down, soon all a girl will be wearing is a belt!" he said, only half joking. "I'm an old man, and I had to turn my head to keep my eyes from looking at the girls' cleavages, exposed midriffs, and legs. I can only imagine what was going on in the minds and bodies of the younger men in the congregation."

My grandmother spoke up. "In defense of our girls, I have to say it's becoming more and more difficult to find youthful clothes that are not tight fitting or revealing. A girl who wants to dress modestly has to work hard to find something suitable yet fashionable in today's stores. I'm not saying it can't be done; it just takes some effort."

She went on. "Oftentimes, a girl won't make that extra effort because she doesn't see why it's necessary. In her mind, she's simply dressing like her friends and trying to get attention from boys. What she doesn't realize is that the more skin she shows, the more enticing she is—that a guy's interest in her can become mostly sexual. My mother used to tell me, 'If you *entice* a man, you'll only have a partner for a night. If you know how to *attract a man the right way*, you'll gain a partner for life one day. He'll want to marry you, not just sleep with you.'" How I loved listening to my grandmother's wise words!

Before calling Jenny, I took a moment to pray for the girls in our groups. I asked for them to receive clear guidelines from our lesson that night regarding what they should or should not be wearing. I prayed they'd be given the grace to dress stylishly, yet modestly—to realize there's a difference between looking enticing and looking attractive. I prayed they'd respect themselves and honor God enough to make changes where necessary. When I finished my prayer, I called Jenny to tell her about David and me.

"I was hoping to talk to you," she said, happy I'd called. "From what John and I saw in church this morning, you have something to tell us."

"Well, as you probably guessed, David and I are officially dating! Actually, he asked Dad for permission to court me."

"That's even better, Julia! Courting leads to marriage, and you couldn't have found a better guy."

"I agree. He's amazing!"

"That's what you're supposed to think. Remember when all of us were vacationing at the cottage before John and I left for Chile? You had just come home from Tyler and were missing having a boyfriend after breaking up with Jay."

"I was pretty miserable, wasn't I?"

"That's an understatement! You were feeling very sorry for yourself and a little jealous because so many people around you seemed to be paired up."

"You're right. At the time, I knew I wasn't ready to meet my Mr. Right, but my desire to have him in my life was just as strong as ever. Do you remember what you told me, Jen, when we were sitting on the front porch glider, waiting for the sun to rise?"

"I'm not sure. We talked about a lot of things."

"I can't quote the exact words, but you told me to stop feeling sorry for myself and looking sad because it wasn't time for me to meet my guy. You said if I would be happy for others along the way, others would be happy for me when it was my turn."

"A better word might be *ecstatic!* I can't wait to go looking for my bridesmaid dress with you," she teased.

"David gave me a *necklace,* Jenny, not a *ring!*" I laughed.

"Hmm...maybe not yet, but he will. It's obvious he loves you! But David knows how much you want to finish grad school, and he's also busy building his practice now. There's no rush. John and I didn't get engaged right away. Enjoy this time in your life, a time when you can have fun simply being in love."

"Exactly! I'm just excited David's my boyfriend now. When it seemed to be taking forever to meet my guy, I had to fight thoughts like *God has forgotten you, It's never going to happen, You're always going to be alone!*

"I knew in my spirit those words weren't true. That's when I had to rise up and push beyond feelings. I had to choose over and over to trust in God's faithfulness when my circumstances seemed to be shouting defeat. I don't know how many times before meeting David I quoted Hebrews 10:35: 'So do not throw away your confidence; it will be richly rewarded.' Because I didn't throw away my confidence in God, I'm finally experiencing the answer to my prayers."

"I can relate, Julia. Those same fearful thoughts played in my head before I met John. I think many singles have to fight them off while waiting for the right person to come along. Hold on a second...I've got to go, Julia. I hear Magda calling; she must be waking up from her nap. See you at church soon?"

"Yes, I'll be there. Bye, little mama."

I hung up the phone, glad to have been able to tell Jenny my great news. Then I stopped and thought about what she'd said last. *See you at church soon.* I looked at my watch. Service was starting in an hour, and David was picking me up in twenty minutes. It was time to ask God for another miracle—being ready on time.

Chapter 15

Think It Through

The next day when I got off work, I came home to change and grab something to eat before my evening class. No cars were in the garage, meaning my parents weren't home from the office yet. Kitty was busying herself in the kitchen when I walked in. We chatted briefly while I sampled some of her freshly baked oatmeal cookies.

"Your young man called about a half hour ago," she informed me. "He said to tell you he was working with Dr. Feinberg tonight, that he'd call you when he got home if it wasn't too late. He said he'd tried to reach you on your cell but couldn't get through."

Apparently, I'd forgotten to charge my phone again. Reaching into my purse, I pulled it out and marched into the mudroom to hook it up. I didn't want to miss *any* of David's calls.

Walking back through the kitchen, I let Kitty know I'd be up in my room if she needed me. As I passed through the foyer, the doorbell rang. When I opened the door, a young man placed a long rectangular box in my arms. "Delivery for Julia Duncan. Sign here, please."

Balancing the box under one arm, I took his pen and signed the receipt on his clipboard. "Thank you," I said before shutting the door.

I already knew from the shape of the box what must be inside. Walking over to the stairs, I sat down and removed the lid. I was right: my eyes beheld twelve beautiful red roses. How sweet of David to order them a second time!

I was anxious to read his card, but I had trouble finding it. Eventually, I saw it had fallen alongside the tissue paper in the box. Wanting to keep the envelope as a keepsake, I carefully opened it to read the card:

> *Julia,*
> *Sorry the delivery of your roses has taken over two weeks. You already know why I'm sending them. I love you with all my heart. Thanks for loving me, too.*
> *David*

"You're quite welcome," I softly answered back with a smile. Leaving the box momentarily on the steps, I ran up to my room to get my special vase.

"Our roses have finally arrived," I happily announced. Then I took the vase with me to collect the flowers waiting below. After cutting the stems and putting them in water, I carried my arrangement to Kitty, who had moved into the dining room to place some table linens into the hutch. Seeing the flowers, she remarked, "How lovely, Julia. I assume they're from your young man."

Nodding, I realized this was the second time she had referred to David as my young man. How I loved the sound of it! Kitty had taken many calls for me in the past from Paul, but she had never referred to him as my young man. My mom must have said something to Kitty about David and me. She was so excited for us; I could tell she was having fun watching her daughter fall in love.

Many times girls feel frustrated while waiting to meet the right man. What they may not realize is that their mothers are hurting right along with them. My mom and I were both thrilled to be pain-free for a change.

The next three months were indescribably wonderful. David and I were extremely busy, but blissfully happy. Dr. Feinberg was using David to speak occasionally at weekend seminars, so I worked my schedule around to attend some of them. Not by myself, though. Because they were overnight stays, my dad asked me to take another female along. My mother went once, and my friend Angela came with me two other times.

When some of my friends in grad school heard about it, they couldn't believe their ears. "Why would you do that?" they asked. "You're both adults; you don't need a chaperone!"

They were surprised by my answer. "As much as David and I love each other, if we were away alone, we might be tempted to make choices we'd regret.

Taking someone with us is an easy solution. We're both Christians, but we're also human. We don't want to put unrealistic expectations on each other."

Some people who aren't living for God don't understand the need for restrictions. They think *if it feels good, do it!* Then, when negative consequences follow bad choices, they look for an easy out, often at the expense of others.

I had taken the path of compromise when I was eighteen years old; I didn't want to travel that road again. That's why I also never went to David's condo alone. We had a rule: I only came with someone else and left when that person did. Actually, it worked out great. We had fun game nights at his place several times with John and Jenny, Cassie and Brian, or Flip and Melody. Sometimes all of us showed up, everyone bringing something to eat. It was always a blast.

John and David played racquetball at night occasionally, too. They were very evenly matched. When I didn't have class, I liked to go and watch them play. It was fun seeing David beat John now and then. I rarely could. But mostly, I enjoyed watching them relate like brothers, a blessing they had both missed out on. Their growing friendship made me even more excited for what the future held for David and me.

Christmas was rapidly approaching, yet I still hadn't found the right gift for David. When I told him I needed some ideas, he suggested we have an early dinner together on Friday and then spend the evening shopping downtown.

The city of Weston always did it up big for the holidays. It was fun to meander in and out of the stores, if only to see the lights and decorations adorning the buildings inside and out. By the time we arrived, a beautiful snowfall was coming down, turning everything into a winter wonderland.

Walking hand in hand, we window-shopped for a while before turning into Marlin's Department Store. In the men's department, I made mental notes on what David said he liked.

Passing the jewelry counter on our way out, he stopped to look in the case. Pointing to the top shelf, he asked me if I liked a particular bracelet. Then he saw a ring further down. "That looks a lot like Cassie's ring, doesn't it?"

"Yes, it's very similar. But Brian got hers at a jewelry store in the mall."

"Question: why would a girl want her boyfriend to pick out an engagement ring for her? What if it wasn't the cut she wanted, or she didn't like the way it looked on her finger? She could be stuck wearing something she didn't like for a long time."

"That's true. I think most couples at least look at rings so the guy has some idea of what his girlfriend likes. That's the way Brian and Cassie did it. But he made the final pick all on his own, and she loves what he got her. On the other hand, Melody wanted to go with Flip to pick her ring herself."

"She's a smart girl. Can you imagine what Flip might have picked on his own?"

I laughed. "Why? Can you get diamonds shaped like car parts?"

"That's not too far fetched. A good jeweler can design almost anything."

"Yes, I know," I replied, affectionately patting my pendant. It made him happy I liked it so much. I never took it off except to shower or go to bed.

Turning to the case again, he pointed to a ring. "This one is pretty."

"I like the setting, but the stone's too big."

"What? Since when does a girl think a diamond is too big?"

"Let me show you something," I said, motioning for a clerk to come and assist us. "May I try a few of these on this tray?"

"Certainly," she replied, handing me my first selection.

"Okay, David, here's the ring you liked with the larger stone. See, my hand is small; the ring is too top heavy for me. Unless it's fitted very tightly, it'll be constantly turning to one side or the other."

Returning the ring to the clerk, I pointed out another ring. After slipping it on, I explained, "Look, this smaller stone is just as pretty and a better balance for the size of my hand. It looks like I'm wearing a ring. The other one looks like the ring is wearing me." David laughed at my analogy. Just for fun, I tried on several others, but I ended up liking the first one the best.

"You seem to prefer this cut," he noticed.

"I guess it's always been my favorite."

"It looks good on you."

"I think so," I agreed.

Thanking the clerk, I let her know we were finished and turned to David. "I've got plenty of ideas for your gift now. Let's go back to my house and watch a movie. I'll make some popcorn if you want. I even have some chocolate we can melt and drizzle over it."

Thirty minutes later, we were sitting in my family room. Our house looked totally different from when I'd left for work that morning; my parents had been putting up Christmas decorations all day. When they decided to go to bed early, I wasn't surprised; they both looked exhausted.

"So, you want the popcorn I was talking about?" I asked once my parents had gone upstairs.

"I don't really want any. In fact, instead of watching a movie, I'd rather sit and talk."

"Okay, follow me."

"Where to?"

"You'll see."

Taking David by the hand, I led him to the couch in the living room. Before sitting beside him, I lit the fireplace, darkened the room, and turned on the Christmas lights, both on the tree and on the wreath over the mantle.

"Nice," he remarked, drinking in the atmosphere.

By then I had joined him. "This is a Duncan tradition at Christmastime, sitting and talking like this."

"It's a good one, Julia, very peaceful. A perfect setting for what I want to say. But first I need a kiss."

And what a kiss it was, the kind that leaves you wanting more. When we both returned to earth, David said tenderly, "You know how much I love you, Julia, so this won't come as any surprise. More than anything, I want you to be my wife. But before I talk to your dad or propose, I want to explain what being married to me would be like.

"The wives of service professionals—like pastors, firemen, or doctors like me—have one thing in common: never having their husbands' complete time and attention. They're often asked to share their husbands with people in crisis. Sometimes that sharing comes at inopportune times: in the middle of the night, holidays, birthdays, anniversaries, or just when you're leaving to go somewhere.

"When I saw you for the first time at the Center, my heart skipped a beat. '*She's the one,*' I heard the Lord say. When I got home that night, I read my Bible and prayed. I felt the Holy Spirit leading me to Proverbs 19:14, which says: 'Fathers can give their sons an inheritance of houses and wealth, but only the LORD can give an understanding wife.'

"Picturing you in my mind, I closed my eyes and waited for the Lord to speak to me. Once again, my spirit heard Him say, '*She's the one.*' I had waited for years to have Him point out the right girl for me. Now I was excited to get to know you. As I was praying about how to approach you, the Lord said to take things *very* slow, not to show any romantic interest until He released me.

"That was no easy assignment. You're a beautiful woman, and I was attracted to you from the start. I don't know if you were counting, but it was five long months before I felt a release to kiss you. By then I wasn't just attracted to you; I was deeply in love. You'll never know the self-control it took to restrain myself, Julia.

"Reflecting, I can see the wisdom in God's plan. Holding back gave us both a chance to really get to know each other before falling off the deep end. You've also had a chance to get a taste of the demands that go along with my profession. So far, you've taken it all in stride without resenting the times I've had to abruptly leave you to go treat a patient. But what you've experienced up until now will intensify after we're married. You'll be done with school by then and working days. That means you'll feel my absences even more if they come up at night or on the weekends, leaving you home alone.

"I want you to think it through, Julia, long and hard. Honestly ask yourself if you can be happy married to a doctor, knowing some of the sacrifices you'll be asked to make. Remember, once we're married, there's no turning back."

I didn't hesitate to answer him. "I've already thought all this through, David; my heart is sure. I'd rather share you than not have you at all. I'm proud of what you do, and I know you. You'll do your best to work out a schedule to be at home as much as you can."

He took me in his arms and kissed me again. Smiling, he said, "It looks like your dad and I will be having lunch again soon."

In all the times I'd been with David, I had never talked about my unfortunate experience with Jay. It wasn't that I was trying to keep it from him. Truthfully, it had happened so long ago, I barely thought about it anymore. But now that we were discussing marriage, it was time for me to tell him.

"There's something you should know about me, David, before you talk to my father."

He listened attentively to the whole story. "I'm still a virgin," I added, "but that guy did try to rape me twice. In doing so, he robbed me of some of my innocence. I wanted you to know all this before you asked me to marry you."

Holding me close, he assured me, "I'm very glad he didn't succeed, more for your sake than mine. But it wouldn't have made any difference to me, Julia, if he *had* succeeded. I love you, and nothing that happened to you in your past could ever change the way I feel about you."

Relieved, I put my head on his shoulder. "Thank you. I love you even more for that!"

We sat there watching the fire until David noticed how late it was. He'd been up since five that morning; I could tell he was tired. We decided to call it a night, and I walked him to the door.

When you're in love, your heart never wants to say goodbye, even when your body is crying out for sleep. The only payback for exercising common sense is a final farewell kiss, which I got before he left.

A Different Christmas

Being on winter break felt wonderful—more time to sleep in, shop, and see my man in the evenings. I was both excited and nervous about the holidays. David was spending Christmas in Weston with me, and then we were going to Baymont the following day so I could meet his parents. I got butterflies in my stomach every time I thought about it. There was no reason to think they wouldn't like me. Still, I had jitters about going.

When Christmas Eve rolled around, my nerves gave way to excitement. My family always went to the six o'clock candlelight service at church. Afterwards, we came home and set out a variety of hors d'oeuvres and homemade Christmas cookies on a table in the living room to snack on while we opened gifts. My grandparents were with my uncle's family this year,

but John, Jenny, and Magda were coming—and David, of course.

He was right when he said we would be having a lot of firsts. I started keeping a record in my journal, listing everything we were doing together for the first time since receiving my necklace. Now we were experiencing our first Christmas together. Knowing my dad had gone out to lunch with David earlier in the week, I was hoping to receive an engagement ring as one of my gifts.

Once John's family arrived after church and we were all seated in the living room, my brother and I passed out the gifts from under the tree. We explained to David that it was our custom for one person at a time to open one gift, taking turns until all the gifts were eventually opened. That way we could enjoy seeing what everyone was getting.

We had to modify our tradition for Magda's benefit because it was already past her bedtime. We let her open all of her gifts first so Jenny could put her to bed in the guest room. Magda was reluctant to leave her new treasures until we reminded her that more gifts were coming in the morning. Pacified, she tucked a new baby doll under her arm and raced off to bed. Once she was tucked in, we adults had our turn.

As usual, everyone loved what he or she received. I deliberately saved the small box from David for last, certain it was my ring. When I removed the top, instead of a ring, I saw the bracelet I had admired at Marlin's. Not wanting to show my disappointment, I graciously thanked David and gave him a kiss. Since my bracelet was the last gift to be opened, we all started cleaning up the paper mess. Then we visited and snacked some more.

Soon John and Jenny decided to leave. They wanted Magda to wake up in her own bed in the morning, excited to open the gifts under their tree. My parents helped Jenny gather their things while John warmed up the car. Once they were gone, my parents excused themselves and retired for the night.

When we were alone, David suggested we sit on the couch in front of the fire. Before sitting down, I turned off all but the Christmas lights in the room and tossed another log on the fire. When I eventually scooted in beside David, I got the kiss I'd been waiting for all night.

"Do you like your bracelet?" he asked.

"You know I do. You wouldn't be fishing for another thank you, would you?"

"I would," he admitted, raising his eyebrows.

Giving him another big kiss, I thanked him again. For the next few minutes, we sat watching the fire together, soaking in the perfection of the moment. Then David surprised me by gently pulling away. "Actually, you have one more gift to open," he said, getting off the couch. Reaching into his pocket, he drew out a ring case. Then he bent down on one knee. My eyes grew wide in anticipation.

"Julia, this is a special moment for me. Though it wasn't easy, with God's help, I've waited and kept myself only for you. You're the answer to my prayers in every way, and I want to spend the rest of my life with you. Will you marry me?"

Elated, I threw my arms around his neck. "Yes, David, I'll marry you."

Pulling back, he smiled before kissing me long and tenderly. When our lips parted, he reminded me, "You haven't looked at your ring yet."

Once he was sitting beside me, I opened the case. My jaw dropped in amazement at what was inside. "David, this is the most beautiful ring I've ever seen! It isn't like any of the ones we looked at together. Where did you find it?"

"Before I tell you, let's get it on your finger." Slipping it on, he remarked proudly, "It's perfect for your hand, isn't it?"

"Yes, perfect, and beyond my wildest expectations. I love it, and I'm so glad you picked it out yourself."

"Actually, I got the idea for the design from the rings you tried on at Marlin's. I went back to the same jeweler where I got your necklace, and he worked overtime getting it ready for me by today."

"May I thank you again?"

"You bet," he said, leaning over to receive my kiss. Then he went on. "You were so gracious when you opened your bracelet tonight. You thought it was your ring, didn't you?"

"Yes, but I didn't want to hurt your feelings by acting disappointed."

"I'm sorry, babe; I just didn't want to give it to you in front of your family. I had their cooperation though.

They agreed to give us some time alone tonight so I could pop the question."

"I'm glad you waited. It was very romantic this way."

"At lunch the other day, your dad gave us his blessing. Later that afternoon, your mom told me your ring size. They said once we were engaged, I should call them by their first names. It's going to feel awkward at first."

I thought, *Not as awkward as I feel about meeting your parents for the first time.* But I didn't share that with David. We were both too happy to think about anything but each other.

After David left, I practically floated upstairs. My ring was so beautiful, I couldn't stop looking at it. I slipped it off briefly while removing my makeup and brushing my teeth, but as soon as I was done, it was back on my finger. Holding out my hand, I admired it under different lights: first in the bathroom, then in my room, and finally under the lamp on my night table. When I calmed down enough to finally fall asleep, the ring was still on; I couldn't bring myself to take it off.

When young children awake on Christmas morning, they rush downstairs, excited to open their presents. When I awoke, I experienced a similar thrill. Flipping off the covers, I stepped into my slippers and ran to find my parents and show them my engagement ring.

I will always remember the wonderful way they received the news. They were not only happy for me, but for David as well. They loved him, too. It was so important to me to have my parents' approval regarding the man I wanted to marry.

I was hoping David's dad and mom would feel the same about me. They were naturally disappointed because he stayed in Weston for Christmas Day, but once he explained to his father that he was getting engaged, his dad said he understood and made David promise to bring me with him when he came home.

The rest of the day, I became left-handed, proudly displaying my ring to the rest of my family at Christmas dinner. David and I received everyone's blessing—things couldn't have gone better!

By the time we left for Baymont the next day, Brian and Cassie knew about our engagement and had offered their congratulations. It had taken me hours to select my clothes and pack for our trip because I wanted to make the very best impression.

David and I had such fun on the ride down. He could make me laugh over the smallest things. We had brought some snacks with us so we could drive straight through. The countryside was snow covered, making the scenery as picturesque as a Currier & Ives painting.

When I eventually saw a sign for Baymont, the butterflies in my stomach returned. David must have sensed I was starting to get nervous because he looked over at me and gave me that reassuring smile of his which I loved so much.

"Our house is about a mile down this way," David announced, making a turn before entering the

Baymont business district. Looking out the window, I observed one stately residence after another along the winding road. They were set back in some of the most gorgeous acreage I had ever seen. "These homes are fabulous, David! Oh, look at that one," I said, pointing to a mansion just ahead of us.

"Let's take a closer look," he suggested. As he slowed down, I was able to make out the engraving on one of the brick pillars at the entrance. I couldn't believe my eyes when I saw the name: **STANTON**.

"This is your parents' house?" I asked in shock as he started up the drive.

"Yep," he answered, matter-of-factly. "Don't let the size intimidate you, Julia. This place collects dust like any other house."

"Oh, I feel sick, David. I want to go home."

Laughing, he reminded me, "Too late. You said you'd marry me, and I'm holding you to your promise. I can't help it that my father has money and my mother likes to flaunt it. If it were up to my dad and me, we'd be living much simpler."

Pointing to the right, I asked, "Are those stables over there?"

"Yes. That's part of the reason my mother wanted this place. Carrie loved horses and was an award-winning equestrienne. She and Cynthia competed together all over the country."

When the car finally stopped on the circular drive in front of the house, I took a deep breath. There was no turning back. David went around and opened my door. Helping me out of the car, he pulled me close and kissed me. "They're going to love you, Julia."

Taking me by the hand, he walked me up the front steps and opened the huge, glass-paneled wooden door. "We're here," he called out once we were inside. I was awestruck by my surroundings. The foyer was huge and regal: marble floor, crystal chandeliers, and expensive furnishings.

While I was admiring the expansive, curved mahogany stairway climbing to the upper level, two figures emerged from a side room. David unclasped my hand to go greet them. Leading them over to where I stood, he introduced me, "Mother, Dad, this is Julia."

They both embraced me, and I felt warmly received. William Stanton was tall and very distinguished looking. As we stood talking, I could see David had gotten his wit and delightful smile from his father. Gloria Stanton was attractive, smartly dressed, and sophisticated in her mannerisms.

"Where's the dog?" Mr. Stanton inquired.

"Since we're only here two nights, I left Sandy at home and hired the boy next door to take care of her."

"Thank goodness," his mother replied, relieved. She excused herself and stepped to the other side of the room for a moment to use the intercom. Returning, she informed us, "We're having lunch in the atrium."

Responding to her call, a man appeared from a hallway behind us and offered to take our coats. "Get Mr. David's keys and bring in their bags, Rodney," Mrs.

Stanton requested. "The young lady will be staying in the larger guest room on the north end. Please take her things up directly."

"Julia's bags are the two blue ones, Rodney," David told him.

"Now let's eat," Mr. Stanton proposed, offering his arm to me. "You escort your mother in, David. Julia and I want to get acquainted."

David's father and I chatted effortlessly as we walked through the house, putting my heart at ease. So far, everything was going fine. I had apparently worried for nothing.

When we reached the atrium, I was taken aback by its amazing décor, similar to an elaborate sunroom I had once seen in a movie. Turning to Mrs. Stanton, I complimented her on her taste.

"The credit is not all mine," she confessed. "I had the help of my gifted decorator, Cynthia Easton. She's like my own daughter, and I'm proud to say her clientele includes many of the most prominent families in Baymont."

David's father raised a brow as if to say, "Spare us, dear." He seated me at the round glass table that had been elegantly set for our luncheon. Mrs. Stanton stepped away to use the intercom before rejoining us. When she saw her husband take the seat beside me, she corrected him, "That's my place, Bill. You're over here."

"Nonsense, Gloria. Come sit between your son and me. David I and both want to be next to Julia." Reaching over to pat my hand, he remarked, "I never pass up a chance to sit next to a beautiful woman. I'm a lucky man today. I have one on either side of me."

He smiled at his wife only to get a cool response to his compliment. Seemingly unaffected, he looked at David and warned him, "Now that Julia is going to be part of our family, you can't keep her all to yourself, son."

Amused, David answered, "I'll try to remember, Dad."

Our table was situated next to an expansive panel of windows showcasing the private lake on the Stanton property. It was still snowing outside, making the scenery even lovelier. On an inner wall, a lit fireplace added just the right warmth and ambiance to the room.

Soon a middle-aged woman in uniform rolled in a serving cart. After filling our glasses with iced tea, she placed a steaming bowl of soup before each of us. David's father prayed, and then we began eating.

During our meal, which turned out to be much more than soup, the Stantons took turns inquiring about my family, schooling, and interests. Mr. Stanton insisted I call them both by their first names.

David's father appeared to be delighted with me as his son's prospective bride. His mother, however, was much harder to read. She was polite but distant. I was proud to show her my engagement ring when she asked to see it, but though she didn't say so, I could tell from the look she gave David, she wasn't impressed.

Once we finished eating, David took me on a tour of the house, all *four* levels. I could see why the Stantons needed an intercom system. One could easily get lost in that mansion! I counted ten bedrooms, each with a private bath. My room was on the far north end of the hall.

My eyes widened when I walked into my quarters. This was some guest room! Actually, it was a luxurious private suite, complete with a fireplace and sitting room. The bathroom was amazing, too, with its huge glass shower, Jacuzzi tub, and lighted dressing table.

"Would you like to rest before dinner?" David offered.

"Sounds great. I can try out that bathtub and nap for a while."

"Okay, sleep well. I'll see you around six."

"You'd better come and get me. I'm not sure I can find my way to the dining room."

"Bribe me," he said, drawing me into his arms and giving me a tender kiss.

Before he left, I had to ask, "Do you think your parents like me?"

"Well, my dad certainly does; I think I may have a rival! As for my mother, who knows what's going on inside her head? I wish you could've known her before Carrie died, Julia. She was such a sweet and charming woman. These days, I'm not sure if she likes anyone, including herself. I barely know her anymore...Please don't worry about her." Giving me a parting kiss, he smiled and reminded me, "Sandy and I love you; that's all that matters. We're the ones you're going to be living with. See you in a few hours."

Dinner that night was very formal. I was glad I had dressed up. After another delicious meal, we all adjourned to the living room so the Stantons could celebrate a belated Christmas.

Though our surroundings were magnificent, from the expensive furniture to the elaborately decorated tree that reached to the top of the cathedral ceiling, the atmosphere was devoid of genuine holiday cheer. The only vitality in the room was coming from the crackling logs in the fireplace. I was certain eating hors d'oeuvres and cookies in this part of the house would be strictly forbidden.

Very few gifts were under the tree, which surprised me considering the Stantons' obvious wealth. Not counting the ones David and I brought, each of us had two gifts apiece. David's father handed him an envelope, which I assumed contained money. David inserted it into his suit pocket without even opening it.

Unlike our tradition, each person opened up all of his or her gifts at once. Being the guest, I was asked to start. I selected the smaller box first. It was so elegantly wrapped, I hated to rip the paper. David reached over and gave it a yank, solving my dilemma.

A lovely cashmere sweater was inside. When I thanked the Stantons, I got a smile from David's father and only a slight nod from his mother. The second gift was in a large box. I couldn't imagine what it could be. I still didn't know once I had it opened.

"It's a riding habit," Mrs. Stanton informed me. "You do ride, of course?"

"No, I'm afraid I don't, Gloria."

"How sad for David. He's a wonderful horseman."

David quickly came to my defense. "I don't have much time for riding these days, Mother. But when we're here, I'll be glad to teach Julia how to handle a horse if she wants to learn."

Trying to be gracious, I held the jacket up to me. The sleeves were noticeably too long, as were the trousers.

"Oh my, I see I guessed your size wrong," Mrs. Stanton remarked. "Having never met you before, I naturally assumed you would be taller. David's other girlfriends have always been tall."

David had an instant response. "You mean the ones *you* tried to match me up with, Mother?"

She remained unfazed by his displeased tone. "Speaking of girlfriends," she continued, "Cynthia was asking about you at the club the other day."

David didn't even acknowledge her last statement with a reply. Looking away from her, he said, "Open your gifts now, Dad."

Bill purposely saved mine for last. "What a nice sweater," he remarked after lifting the lid and flipping the tissue paper aside. "I love it, Julia. Thank you."

"Bill, what do you think you're doing?" Gloria scolded, embarrassed at seeing him remove his suit coat and tie.

"I'm trying on my sweater, dear."

"Must you do it now?"

"No time like the present," he answered. Once it was on, he announced it fit fine. Then he came over and sat beside me on the couch, giving me a sweet kiss on the cheek. "Your turn," he said, gesturing to his son.

While David was opening his gifts, I was stressing. His mother was going to be next. I had picked out a lovely silk blouse for her from Marlin's that I really liked. I wasn't worried about it fitting because David had given me her size. But now, after meeting her, I wasn't sure how she would feel about receiving something from a lowly department store.

All too soon, the moment arrived, and she was opening my gift. She deliberately looked at the name on the lid before removing it. "Marlin's?" she said as though she had never heard of the store. "Is that where you shop, dear?"

"Sometimes," I answered, feeling self-conscious.

Separating the tissue paper, she looked inside the box. "How sweet," she remarked, indifferently. Looking at the label in the collar to check the size, she added, "I'm sure it will fit. Thank you."

"You're welcome," I replied, certain that as soon as I had gone back home, this beautiful blouse would find its way into one of her charity bins.

Since all the gifts had been opened, I got up and started collecting the discarded wrapping paper. Mrs. Stanton stopped me. "Don't bother, Julia. That's why we have a maid. Bessie will take care of that tomorrow." Once again, I had been reproved by her condescending tone. Clearly, the Stantons celebrated

a different Christmas than the Duncans. I much pre-
ferred ours.

David came over and gave me an affectionate hug
as if apologizing for his mother. Then he suggested
we go into the theater room and watch a movie. Mr.
Stanton thought that was a great idea, but his wife
excused herself. She said she had a headache and
wanted to retire. I couldn't help but wonder if *I* were
the headache she was trying to escape. It's not very
nice to say, but she wasn't missed. The three of us had
much more fun the rest of the evening without her.

After the movie, I said good night to Mr. Stanton,
and David walked me to my room. He stepped inside
for a brief moment to say he felt terrible about the
way his mother was behaving. "I can't believe she's
acting like this toward you," he said, both upset and
disappointed.

I put my arms around his waist, my head resting
on his chest as we stood together. Needing to say
something, I looked up at him. "I don't mean to criticize your mom, honey, but honestly, she doesn't treat
you or your dad much better than she treats me. Why
do you both let her get away with it?"

"Because it's easier to ignore her than to confront
her. Trust me, she has a way of making you pay for it
if you try."

"Avoidance may be easier, David, but you aren't
doing yourselves or her any favors. You're only
reinforcing her bad behavior. It's the truth that sets
people free."

"I'm sure you're right, Julia. After Carrie died, Dad and I babied her too much. Maybe if we'd helped her face reality from the very beginning, she wouldn't have turned to medication to deal with her pain."

"The drugs may be helping her pain, David, but we both know they can negatively alter a person's personality. I've seen it happen over and over at the Center."

"Of course I know that, Julia. But I can't make her follow my recommendations."

"No, you're right. That's your father's responsibility. But it's hard to show tough love to someone you pity. Your mother doesn't need his pity; she needs his help."

David looked at me as though a light had gone on in his mind. "My dad and I have been praying wrong," he said, "simply asking *God* to help her deal with her grief while sitting back and waiting for it to happen, not realizing that all our indulgences have only been compounding her problem. Maybe God wants to use us to help her in a different way…Thanks for being so honest, Julia. I need to think about this."

Kissing me one last time, he left to go to his room down the hall. Once I was ready for bed, I prayed for all the Stantons before falling asleep—and for the grace to face Gloria again at breakfast.

The Unexpected

I slept restlessly all night, probably from the emotional strain of meeting David's mother. In the morning, the sound of someone knocking on my door awakened me. Scrambling, I grabbed my robe lying across the foot of the bed. Thinking it might be David, I quickly ran my fingers through my hair to look more presentable before answering the door.

Much to my surprise, it was Bessie, the Stantons' maid. "Sorry to disturb you, Miss, but Mr. David asked me to tell you breakfast is being served in an hour in the atrium."

"Thank you," I replied. "I'll start getting ready."

The hot water from the pulsating showerhead felt wonderful, but I couldn't take time to indulge in a prolonged water massage. I needed to hurry in order to be dressed and downstairs on time. I certainly didn't want to give David's mother any further reasons to criticize me.

"Stop worrying," I quietly scolded myself. "You are not going to cave in to Gloria's whims the way David and his dad do." Thinking that through, I slowed down. I wasn't trying to be late, but I wasn't about to be manipulated by Gloria's childish behavior either. I would do my best, and that would have to be enough.

Exactly one hour and six minutes later, I left my room. David was patiently waiting for me at the bottom of the stairs with an embrace and a good morning kiss.

Thankfully, Gloria seemed to be in better humor at breakfast. I rather enjoyed our conversation. Bill, as I was reminded twice to call him, was his charming self.

David and I were both dressed in jeans and sweaters since we'd made plans the night before to walk over to the stables and see the horses. When we finished eating, David took me by the hand and told his parents where we were going.

"Don't keep her out there too long," Gloria requested. "I'd like to spend some time with Julia this afternoon, and she'll need to change clothes. We're having lunch together at the club, so you and your father will be on your own. If you won't be here at noon to eat, please tell Wilma not to prepare anything. Dinner will be at seven."

I wasn't sure how I felt about my luncheon date, considering I hadn't been asked to go, that my consent was merely assumed. In an effort to be positive, I chose to see it as a good sign: my future mother-in-law was attempting to get to know me better.

David and I bundled up before walking out of the house and trudging along the wooded path to the stables. The Stantons had four horses; I met Triumph and Lady Beth first. They were used primarily for guests, although David said his parents rode them occasionally—not so much in recent years. Then I met David's horse, Charger. He told me the horse had been appropriately named because he would often take flight when spooked. Finally, I met Majesty, Carrie's horse.

"Cynthia's the only one my mother will allow on Majesty since Carrie's death," he explained. "She comes out here often so the horse can be exercised. My mother should sell Majesty. Seeing her only brings back painful memories."

While we were in the stables, I met Kurt, the groom for the horses. As he stood talking to David, I reviewed in my mind the servants the Stantons employed: a driver, a butler, two maids, a cook, and a groomsman. I was sure they also had a gardener during the summer. That came to at least seven. I smiled when I thought about Cassie. She had always been impressed because my parents employed Kitty, who served as a combination maid/cook three times a week. The Stantons' setup would really blow Cassie away.

When David and I returned to the house, it was already time for me to get changed for my outing with his mother. I quickly showered again to remove any possible stable smell. Then I picked out an appropriate outfit and reapplied my makeup. When I was finished, I was confident even Gloria couldn't find fault with the way I looked.

David was standing in the foyer talking with his mother when I came downstairs. Neither of them looked happy. I had interrupted a heated discussion about something, hopefully not about me. I had no idea where I stood with Gloria Stanton, if she even liked me.

"There you are," she said, turning to greet me, smiling politely as though nothing were wrong. "Shall we go?"

When David leaned down and kissed me goodbye, I thought I saw Gloria wince out of the corner of my eye. Or was that only my imagination?

Their driver had brought the car around and parked it out front. As we walked down the front steps, he politely opened my door for me. Gloria informed him he was no longer needed as she slid behind the wheel herself.

She did most of the talking as we drove into town. She proudly named several of the families who lived in the estates along the way. "We're all members of the same country club," she bragged. "Before we have lunch, I need to stop and pick up a prescription."

I expected to drive up to a drug store somewhere in town, but instead we pulled into the parking lot of a huge medical facility—Bradley Health Center. Gloria invited me to come in with her.

"What a beautiful building," I observed once we were inside.

"Yes, it is," she answered in a frustrated tone. "This is where David *should* be practicing medicine under a respected physician like Winston Bradley, not in some one-horse town like Weston, certainly not with a quack like Neil Feinberg."

Since David had already told me his mother didn't like his professional choices, I wasn't surprised by her disapproving words. Fortunately, I didn't have to reply to her snide comment; we had arrived at the pharmacy, and her attention was immediately diverted.

Once we were back in the car, Gloria asked me, "Did you know Dr. Bradley wanted David to stay in Baymont, that he offered him a very prestigious position in his practice?"

"No, I didn't," I honestly replied.

"Well, he did, but David didn't appreciate what an honor that was. In time, I believe David will get all this natural medicine foolishness out of his head and come to his senses. Once he does, he can come back home and make the most of his career."

I couldn't keep silent any longer. "Gloria, David believes he's doing that already."

"I see he's got you brainwashed, too," she said, annoyed.

Certain it was a waste of time trying to reason with her, I didn't pursue the subject any further. On the way to the country club, Gloria drove slowly past the Stantons' family-owned bank. "This is our main

branch," she informed me. "We have thirty other branches scattered throughout Baymont and the surrounding communities."

Driving on from there, she chattered away about her involvement in church and community affairs. It was a one-sided conversation, my part being a listener only. I couldn't imagine why Gloria had wanted us to have lunch together. It was clear she had no genuine interest in finding out more about me.

The country club was exactly as I had pictured it, extremely high-end, designed to cater to the very rich. When we entered the dining room, Gloria stopped to greet several people without even bothering to introduce me. I felt invisible.

Then the unexpected happened. The hostess led us to a table where a very beautiful, well-dressed young woman was sitting. Before we sat down, Gloria walked over and gave her a hug. "Wonderful to see you, Cynthia," she expressed, warmly. "I'm so glad you could make it on such short notice." Gesturing to me, she added, "Oh, yes, this is Miss Duncan. She is staying with us for the weekend."

There was no mention of David or the fact that we were engaged. Extending my hand to Cynthia, I said, "Hi, Cynthia. I'm Julia, David's fiancée. I've heard so much about you. It's nice to finally meet you."

My news noticeably shocked her. When Gloria arranged that luncheon, she had apparently neglected to tell Cynthia that she was bringing David's fiancée along. I felt sorry for both her and me. Gloria, however, appeared to be enjoying our awkward meeting. I knew David thought of Cynthia as a sister, but that didn't mean she felt the same way about him. When she heard we were engaged, I couldn't tell if her reaction reflected jealousy or merely surprise.

Once Gloria and I were seated, the three of us sat silently at the table for a moment. I smiled at Gloria and Cynthia and then picked up the large menu before me, thankful for something to do. The tension in the air was momentarily broken when our waitress arrived to take our orders.

For the duration of the meal, I was virtually ignored. Cynthia tried several times to include me in the conversation, but Gloria skillfully drew her away from me by discussing subjects she knew I had little experience or knowledge of—event decorating, horseback riding, or local community happenings. Whenever I tried to initiate conversation myself, Gloria found a reason to interrupt and engage Cynthia without me.

Finally, we were finished eating and stood to leave. I had a chance to quickly look Cynthia over as she hugged Gloria goodbye. Besides being gorgeous, she was very tall and slender, which explained the deliberate comment Gloria had made to me the night before about David preferring taller women. I was sure the riding habit I'd received from her for Christmas would fit Cynthia perfectly. It was never intended to be a gift for me. Instead, it was a subtle message that I was not a right fit for David.

I drew upon my entire wholesome upbringing to get me through that luncheon without showing my exasperation or bursting into tears. It wasn't until Gloria and I were back in her car that I dared to be honest.

Before she pulled the gearshift into drive, I reached over and turned the ignition off. She looked at me in surprise.

"Gloria, can we please talk?" I requested. "There must be a reason for the unkind way you've been treating me today. I think you at least owe me an explanation."

"Very well," she responded, her eyes narrowing. "Since you insist, I'll tell you outright. I don't want you to marry David. He should have brought you home before he impulsively gave you an engagement ring, such as it is. But then David always does exactly what he wants, no matter how much it hurts me. You just met the woman who *should* be David's wife. She's like my own daughter, and I will *never* feel that way about you.

"I can't stop you and David from marrying, but before you do, I wanted to give you a taste of how things will be between us. I'll be civil when my son is around, but when we're alone, I'm going to treat you like you're not even there. You won't get a single kind word from me. Try explaining *that* to your children. My son loves me, so you won't be able to completely avoid being around me. We'll see each other plenty, my dear. If you make life miserable for me with this marriage, then I'll make it even more miserable for you! Think about that before you decide to go ahead and marry David."

I sat there dazed, unable to believe what I was hearing. I had never received such total rejection from anyone in my life. I inwardly prayed for composure and the right words to answer; I didn't want to let David's mother see how deeply her words had hurt me. While I was searching for some reply to her threats, she offered a brief explanation.

"Julia, we barely know each other, so this isn't about you personally. I would feel the same about *any* girl David wanted to marry other than Cynthia. He needs someone like her to help him reach his potential. He's just like his father. If it hadn't been for me, Bill would never be the successful banker he is today. I also know if David marries you, it will keep him in Weston, and my hopes of him returning to Baymont and the life I want for him will be forever lost. I'm not going to let that happen."

Though my heart was crushed, I tried my best to respond to her without being nasty. "You're right about only one thing, Gloria: Everything you said *isn't* about me. It's all about you and what *you* want. With all due respect, do you really believe you have the right to map out David's life for him? He's not your little boy anymore; he's a grown man. Do you want him to be happy or merely under your control? And what about Bill? Do his feelings matter? From what I've seen these last two days, you don't treat him like a loving wife." I cringed at my own last words; I had gone too far with them.

Gloria indignantly turned on the ignition before answering, "What goes on between my husband and me is none of your business. As far as I'm concerned, this conversation is over!"

I felt exactly the same. Neither of us said anything else on the ride back to the Stantons'. When we arrived, Gloria parked the car in front of the house, removed her keys, and went inside ahead of me. By the time I reached the foyer, I could see her climbing the stairs, most likely on the way to her room.

Then I saw David walking toward me. "Welcome home, babe. I missed you. Did you and my mother have fun?" he asked, expecting good news. When he was near enough to read the expression on my face, he knew something had happened. "What's wrong, Julia? You look upset."

"We have a serious problem," I said blinking back tears, refusing to cry.

"We can't talk here—let's go into the library."

Once there, David closed the door behind us, and we sat together on the leather couch facing the fireplace. After I told him about our lunch with Cynthia, relaying my conversation with his mother in the car, he stood and began to pace back and forth, furious. He vented for a few minutes, sharing his shock and frustration at his mother's inexcusable behavior.

Before anything else was said, I had to know something. "David, you told me Cynthia was like a sister, but is it possible she's in love with you?"

"No way, Julia. When Carrie died, Cynthia was invited over here a lot. We both missed my sister and did spend a lot of time together exercising the horses, talking and reminiscing about Carrie. But the only romance between us exists in my mother's mind. It's what she *wants* to believe."

"Have you and Cynthia ever explained to your mom that you're *not* in love, that you're only friends?"

"Several times! But people who are delusional only hear what they want to hear. After a while, we gave up and let her think what she wanted. You should be able to relate to that. Paul was delusional about you; that's why he never accepted the answer *no*. Actually, Cynthia is pretty serious about a guy she met while traveling on business last year."

"I'm happy for her, David, but where does that leave us?"

"I don't understand what you mean."

"As long as your mother feels as she does about me, marriage for us seems out of the question right now."

David looked as though I had knocked the wind out of him. "You can't be serious."

"David, you're forgetting that I'm not only marrying you, but your family as well. These are *your parents*, our kids' *grandparents* one day, and they'll be sharing our lives as long as they live: birthdays, holidays, visits. Even though your father has accepted me, your mother just told me in no uncertain terms that she never would. Her hatred of me would always be a wedge between us and a horrible example of family to our children. This isn't the relationship with a mother-in-law I've been hoping for all these years. I've had enough emotional abuse from your mom this weekend to last a lifetime!"

David began pacing again, running his hands through his hair, trying to process what I'd just said. Finally, he came over, pulled me up into his arms, and held me tight. Pulling back to look at me, he apologized. "I am so sorry to be putting you through all this. I've been living away from my mother for so long, I didn't know how much her condition had deteriorated. When I was home last, other than her reaction to some of the drugs she's taking, she seemed fairly normal."

"That's because she had you where she wants you—at home with her. Plus you weren't openly attacking her obsession to see you and Cynthia together."

"That's probably true, but I'm not going to lose you because of her. I've been waiting too long to find you to let my mother mess this up. I really wish you had known her before Carrie died. She's always been a bit of a snob, but up until then, she was a wonderful, caring mother and so much fun. Are you sure you're not overreacting to some of the things she said today?"

"Hardly, David. She told me she would make my life miserable if I married you."

"Well, that's what she says now, but I'm sure once we're married, she'll come around. Try to remember, she's on so many medications, she doesn't know what she's saying half the time."

"Maybe not, but what she says hurts me deeply, and I don't want to have to go through this over and over. The way things stand, I haven't the slightest hope her feelings will change toward me after we're married."

"I'm so angry with my mother right now, I can't even think!"

"We both need some time to think, David. I'm going up to my room to rest before dinner. Why don't you spend some time talking with your dad about this?"

"I will, Julia. Somewhere in this mess God has an answer for us."

I barely got out the words *I hope so* before he kissed me as though it might be our last kiss. "I love you so much, Julia. You mean everything to me. I can't believe this is happening."

Pulling away, I looked him in the eye. "Believe it—then deal with it! The time for ignoring this problem is over, David. It hasn't worked in the past, so it's not going to work now. This thing has to be met head-on, for your mom's sake as well as for ours. It's something you and your dad have to do. All of the appeasing the two of you have done to make her happy has made it possible for your mom to spoil the happiness of others.

"I hope I don't sound too harsh right now, David. I want this to get resolved for your mom, your dad, *and* us. Life in your family can't go on like this anymore. It hurts everybody. When you talk to your dad, try to remember that being angry with your mom won't accomplish what you want. Whatever is said and done from this point on has to be motivated by love for your mom, no matter how bad she's acting. We know from Scripture that showing goodness to those who don't deserve it can cause a positive change."

David was overwhelmed, but he agreed with me. Minutes later when I got to my room, all my previous emotional reserve gave way to tears. It felt good to finally release them. Yet while I was crying, I wasn't experiencing a sense of total loss, only the realization that a postponement of our marriage was inevitable. My dad's concerns about David's mother had proved to be valid. I loved David with all my heart, but until Gloria's attitude changed toward me, our love would have to be put on hold.

Difficult Assignment

Having finished a good cry on the bed in the Stanton guest room, I got up and washed my face, letting the cool water calm me. Looking at my red-eyed reflection in the mirror, I couldn't believe how much had changed in two short days. All the elation of our engagement was leveled by the realization that David and I had something very serious to work through.

We both believed God had brought us together, yet here we were, facing a huge obstacle, one I sincerely felt had to be removed before we were married. But how? Gloria's emotional problems had only been accelerating over the past five years. It would take all our faith to believe that somehow the tide could be reversed, that things could really change.

A soft knock at the door jarred me out of my musings. I opened the door to find David there, looking more dejected than I had ever seen him. He

stepped into the room, cracking the door behind him. Taking my hand, he led me to the sitting area of the suite, where we sat down together on the linen sofa.

David looked emotionally drained as he explained what had transpired over the last couple of hours. "After you went upstairs, I found my dad and told him what had happened today. I could tell he was embarrassed as well as sad to hear it, but not completely shocked. He knows deep down that my mother is out of control, that she desperately needs help.

"We talked about a few medical options, but we're both too upset right now to make any real decisions. My dad said to tell you he's truly sorry for the hateful things that were said to you. He's really beside himself, struggling to know what to do. But Julia, I want you to know that he's for us. I know he'll act now that he sees how serious this is getting.

"Maybe I shouldn't tell you this, but I went up and spoke with my mother. She denied many of the things she said, of course, accusing you of being immature and insecure, more reasons why marrying you would be a mistake. I've never seen her so unreasonable or heard her outright lie before. She isn't acting like herself at all anymore, and it scares me. No matter what I said, how I explained my love for you, she wouldn't listen. I don't know, Julia. I just have to believe that we can get through this."

It hurt to see David so discouraged. I squeezed his hand and thanked him for tackling this straight on instead of wishing it away as usual. I saw that my words encouraged him little. Neither of us wanted to go down to dinner, but it was almost seven by now with David's parents no doubt waiting for us below.

Fortunately for all of us, Gloria didn't come down for the evening meal but asked for a tray to be sent up to her room instead. I was relieved, grateful not to have to see her again that night.

David's father couldn't have been kinder to me over dinner. He apologized several times for his wife's behavior, obviously dealing with both regret for the situation and concern for my feelings. I assured him I understood how drugs could affect a person's personality, that I had yet to meet the real Gloria Stanton.

Because of the circumstances, the next morning David and I decided to skip church with his parents and leave for Weston first thing. Gloria refused once again to come downstairs for breakfast. When it was time to go, David went up to his mother's room to say goodbye. I never did have to face her after our argument in the car.

David and I talked all the way home, but it didn't accomplish much. All we were doing was rehashing it all. The fact that David's mother lied about what she said and did only confirmed my concerns. We were looking forward to getting my parents' input, to draw upon their wisdom and get a fresh perspective.

As we drove, I kept looking at my engagement ring, aware that until we experienced a breakthrough with David's mother, it would have to come off. I tried my best to hold back the tears, but they kept coming in waves right up until the time we pulled into my driveway.

My parents met us at the door expecting to greet two happy people. Instead, they embraced a heart-broken daughter and future son-in-law. My mom put her arm around me for comfort as my parents led us into the kitchen.

"Let's talk this out over a cup of coffee," my father suggested.

I was still crying as we all sat down at the breakfast nook, so David shared most of what had transpired during our two-day stay with his parents. We could tell my mom and dad were hurting right along with us.

"The two of you have a difficult assignment ahead," my dad said at last. "I agree with Julia, David. Your mother's attitude toward her needs to change before you get married. Otherwise, your chances for happiness will be affected; you'll be constantly dealing with strife within your family.

"Scripture warns us that strife opens the door to bad things. You're the one who will be torn, David, because God asks you to honor your parents as long as they live. Just as importantly, He requires you to love and protect your wife. Since your mother refuses to accept Julia and deliberately treats her so spite-fully, it will be hard for you to fulfill both obligations. One of the women you love will be constantly dealing with hurt feelings.

"Remember when you asked for permission to court Julia? We spent a lot of time talking about your relationship with your parents. You told me that before Carrie died, you and your mom were close.

Even though you're angry with her now, it's obvious how much you love her. I also know you and your dad are close friends. Can you see that marriage for you *must* include an ongoing relationship with your parents? As much as Julia loves you, she wouldn't want to see you turn your back on your family because of her. At the same time, she doesn't want to spend a lifetime dealing with your mother's rejection. Grace and I certainly don't want that for Julia, either. She deserves better."

David's eyes were moist with tears as he listened to my father's words. "I don't understand," he responded, shaking his head. "I know I heard God tell me two different times that Julia was the one for me. I followed His every direction from the time we met, holding back when my heart wanted to show my love for her. I didn't even kiss her until I felt He gave me the go-ahead. Why would He let us fall in love, knowing we couldn't have a future together?"

"He wouldn't," my mom assured him. "I believe that in God's plan, you and Julia are meant for each other."

David reached over and took my hand. Then he looked back at my parents. "She's everything I've prayed for and wanted in a wife. I've ended other relationships through the years because I knew they weren't right. I've waited a long time and worked very hard to be worthy of Julia." Heaving a deep sigh, he continued, "For the first time, I understand how Abraham must have felt when God asked him to offer up Isaac on the altar. That man believed the Lord for a son for twenty-five years, and after he had finally fathered him and was at his happiest, he was asked to kill his dream."

My dad reached over and put his hand on David's shoulder to console him. "I like the word *sacrifice* better than *kill*, David. If you remember the story, Abraham's love for God was being tested, and his willingness to take that test made it possible for him to *keep* his dream.

"You and Julia love each other and want to be together, but someone else has a greater need right now—your mother. I don't presume to know how all this is going to play out in the end, yet I'm sure God is asking you to put your marriage plans on the altar of sacrifice and leave them there until He resolves this problem for you. Doing that will take some time and a lot of faith."

Although I knew I was going to have to postpone my engagement to David, there was something I hadn't considered. "Can we still see each other at least?" I asked my parents, choking back more tears.

"That choice will be up to you two," my mother answered. "But sacrifice requires the giving up of something you value, causing you a certain amount of pain. If you merely return David's ring but continue to see each other like nothing has happened, that's not much of a sacrifice. You're not really taking the faith test being asked of you. Besides, if you go on seeing each other, your love will continue to grow, and you'll want to get married even more than you do now."

"Your mother has a point," my dad agreed. "A love that isn't willing to risk isn't worth having. I speak from experience because your mom and I were kept from seeing each other for eighteen months while God was doing a work in me. We have never regretted making that sacrifice up front."

My dad looked at us with empathy. Reaching for my hand, he said, "I'm not sure if what I'm going to suggest will make sense to your minds, but hopefully, it will to your spirits. If God truly said you and Julia were to be together, David, you can trust Him to make it happen. Faith moves mountains. There isn't any problem too difficult for Him to handle as you trust in His wisdom and ability to make everything turn out better than you can even imagine."

We knew in our hearts my parents were right, but knowing that didn't make it any easier to face what was ahead of us. Saying goodbye to David that afternoon in our foyer was the hardest thing I'd ever done. I'm not sure which of us was more heartbroken. When I slipped off my ring and handed it to him, David took me in his arms and kissed me tenderly.

Then he asked, "Are you sure you want to do this?"

"No," I responded, still in his arms, fighting back more tears. "You know it isn't what I *want* to do, but no matter how hard this is, I believe it's what God is asking us to do."

I barely got the words out before he kissed me again, long and hard. When our lips parted, he looked at me and forced a smile. "Then that kiss will have to last us for a while."

"I know," I replied, trying to stay strong.

"We're going to get through this," he promised, trying to make our parting easier. "We have a lot of great people who will be praying for us. We aren't alone."

I nodded, unable to answer.

"Since we're going to do this, Julia, let's do it right. We'll see each other at church, but I don't think we should sit together. I'll call Jeremy and ask him to take my boys' group for a while. That way we won't have to be around each other at the youth program or leaders' meetings. We're going to need God's grace in the days ahead because we can't totally avoid seeing each other. I have one patient right now at the Center, but she's due to go back home in a few weeks. Once she's gone, you won't have to run into me at work."

Looking up at him, I said softly, "I love you, David. When I do see you, I don't think I'll be able to hide it with my eyes."

"I love you, too, Julia," he replied, cupping my face with his hand, gently stroking my cheek with his thumb. "Don't try to hide it. When we look at each other, we'll be reminded that our love and faith are continuing to work for us so we can be together again soon."

After he left, I went back into the kitchen to be with my parents. I didn't want to be alone. I asked my mom and dad to call John and Jenny as well as Cassie and Brian to tell them what had happened and to get their prayer support. I wasn't ready to talk to anyone myself yet.

Fortunately, David and I had not been in church since he gave me the ring, so nobody besides my family and Brian and Cassie knew we had gotten engaged at Christmas. That spared us having to explain to our friends why we had broken it off. Still, there would be questions about why we were no longer dating. *It's none of your business* would be the easiest response, but not a kind one. I wasn't sure what I was going to tell people.

Melody and Flip were the first to ask. "We've decided to put things on hold," I simply answered. That became my response whenever someone inquired.

Once again, I spent New Year's Eve alone. Things were a little more bearable with John's family around, and I was happy my grandparents were back in town. Of course, I told them both the whole story.

My grandmother truly encouraged me because she offered more than sympathy. Actually, she corrected me when I told her how much I'd been praying for David and me. "You and David aren't the problem, Julia," she pointed out. "It's Gloria Stanton you need to be focusing your prayers on. We want her to be healed, not only because you and David want to be married. This woman is living with a lot of pain and trying to deal with it in her own strength. I sense that she's battling more than the natural grief that comes from losing a child. Something else is tormenting her. God alone knows the root cause of her problem, and I can guarantee you, He's the only One who knows how to solve it.

"We also need to pray for David and his father—for wisdom to know what they should say and do each step of the way toward Gloria's recovery. They both need strength to be able to deal with her in love when she fights their efforts to help her."

Listening to my grandmother, I realized my concern for David's mother was steeped in selfishness. After all, I'd known about her condition for months while David and I fell in love, but I'd never been motivated to pray for her before the breaking of our engagement.

From then on, my prayers changed. Instead of just focusing on my own pain and loss, I actually began to have a genuine compassion for David's mother, what *she* was presently going through. With God's help, I was no longer praying for her just so I could have my heart's desire, but so she could finally be set free.

Even so, I kept hoping everything would be resolved quickly. Yet it wasn't. I had to remind myself daily that miracles are instantaneous, but healings take time. Minutes turned into hours, hours into days, days into weeks. The only diversion from what was going on in my life was the happy anticipation of the arrival of John and Jenny's baby. He came right on schedule in the middle of February, the perfect Valentine's Day present. They named him John Jr., after my brother.

When I arrived at the hospital to see my nephew for the first time, David was in Jenny's room, standing by her bed, congratulating her and John. I walked over and stood beside him while we both admired little Johnny.

Every time we saw each other, it was the same. Our eyes told us what we each wanted to know: *I love you more than ever. I miss you terribly.* We were learning that true love doesn't die, even when it's being starved. It simply continues to grow.

Because we had agreed to sever all romantic ties, we didn't intentionally meet anywhere, text, email, or talk on the phone. Although seeing each other was never planned, David and I lived for moments like these when we could at least be in the same room together. David never looked more handsome to me than when he had on a hospital coat. Perhaps that was because he was wearing one the first time we met.

Neither of us was anxious to end our visit that afternoon. We were savoring every minute of relating back and forth with John and Jenny, but mostly with each other. David was the first to leave.

Before turning to walk out the door, he discretely reached over and gave my hand a squeeze. How I missed his touch. It was almost as good as receiving one of his kisses. Even though it was sort of crossing the boundary line we'd drawn, in my heart, I felt God understood.

My brother and David were still playing racquetball often. It was through John that we each kept up on how the other was doing. All I knew currently about Gloria was that David's father had checked her into an upscale treatment center not far from Baymont.

Like Dr. Feinberg, the doctor who was attending her had adopted many natural methods into his practice, a fact David's father intentionally withheld from his wife.

My life had returned to the way it was before meeting David. I threw myself into work, school, and my girls' ministry at church. My family and friends were very supportive of what David and I were going through. Everyone was praying, and thankfully, nobody was asking questions about our current status. God was in the driver's seat—we were merely passengers along for the ride, confident that the safe arrival to our destination was somewhere down the road. It just had to be.

I spent a lot of my free hours at John's house because I loved being around the children. Six-year-old Magda was a great big sister—such a help to Jenny with the baby. Being an affectionate little girl, I received from her precious hugs and kisses that helped to make up for the attention I was no longer getting from David.

When March rolled around, I got involved with last minute preparations for Melody and Flip's shower and wedding. Every time I did something for my friends, I'd say, "I'm planting a seed. Soon I'll be planning my own wedding." The only question in my mind was *when?*

Tea Party

Like every bride, Melody looked radiant on her wedding day in her elegant gown and veil. She was lovely as she glided into position at the rear of the sanctuary, still out of sight of the guests. Since Melody's sister was her maid of honor, I had light duty as one of four bridesmaids.

When it was my turn to walk down the aisle, I scarcely recognized Flip standing ahead of me. He looked quite handsome in his black tailcoat and pinstriped trousers, traditional dress for a morning ceremony.

As my friends took their vows, tears began to slip down my cheeks. Fortunately, the handkerchief I had wrapped around the stem of my bouquet came to my rescue. A few of the other bridesmaids were crying, too. Onlookers no doubt assumed that, like the others, my tears were brought on by sentiment. But in my case, they were flowing from a broken heart.

Standing diagonally on the platform, watching Flip and Melody exchange rings, I could see David out of the corner of my eye, sitting in the congregation off to my right. Even though I had faith that one day we would be married, at that moment, a feeling of hopelessness swept over me.

I had to remind myself that trusting God didn't mean our separation wouldn't hurt; it just meant the pain would be worth it in the end. I recited *It's worth it!* silently to myself until the lump in my throat went away and I was back in control of my emotions.

Because the reception was a brunch, there was no dancing, only background music. I was happy about that because I would have been tempted to dance with David, to have an excuse to be in his arms again and feel him close to me. How I ached for his embrace!

I was standing up with Melody's older brother, Andrew. Living out east, he had flown in for the wedding, and I had met him for the first time at the wedding rehearsal the previous night. He was a few years older than I was and ran a large contracting business.

From our first introduction, he gave every indication of being attracted to me. His smiles and attentiveness during the rehearsal dinner were proof that I had read him right. Andrew continued to pursue me at his sister's wedding, but while he was quite handsome and charming, someone else had already won my heart.

As we talked, Andrew must have noticed my focus was not on him; it was on David. My eyes continually found him wherever he was sitting or standing, just as his eyes searched out mine across the room. Our only contact came in a few casual conversations, yet it was enough to keep the flame of our love burning. We were enduring the heartache of our separation only because we believed our pain was a faith deposit toward allowing God to reunite us—and once united, never to be separated again.

The only upside to my situation with David was that I was able to spend more time on my studies. I was finishing my third semester of grad school, and what was required of me was steadily intensifying.

By the time summer arrived in June, I was experiencing a lot of emotional pressure. It had been over five months since David and I had broken our engagement. Nothing indicated we were even close to a breakthrough. I daily encouraged myself that breakthroughs often happen suddenly—in ways you least expect. That was what my grandmother had told me anyway. I was hanging on to those words with all my heart.

Driving home from work one Friday afternoon, I was missing David more than usual. Distracted by my thoughts, praying and straining to stay positive, I didn't notice a car parked on the street in front of my house. I merely drove into the garage as usual and came in through the mudroom.

My mother was in the kitchen fixing a pot of tea. She greeted me with a smile before setting the pot on a tray along with two cups, sugar and cream, and a plate of homemade cookies.

"Are we having a tea party?" I asked.

"You are, actually," she responded matter-of-factly. "Someone is here to see you."

"Who?"

"It's a surprise!"

"There are only two cups, Mom. Aren't you joining us?"

"Not this time, Julia. I'm sure your visitor wants to speak with you alone."

Now my curiosity was piqued. I had no idea whom she meant. Picking up the tray, my mother led the way with me following her. As we neared the living room, she looked back at me and whispered, "Prepare yourself, honey."

Rounding the corner, I could see a woman sitting on the sofa with her back to us. When she heard the slight rattling of the cups on the tray, she stood and turned. When I saw her face, I'm sure the color instantly drained from mine as I felt my stomach knot.

Smiling, she immediately came toward me. "I'm so glad to see you again, Julia," she said warmly, reaching to clasp my hand. Giving it an affectionate squeeze, she let it drop and then invited me to sit with her on the sofa for a moment. I obeyed without a word, still in shock. My mother followed and set the tray before us on the coffee table.

"I'll let you two talk," she said before leaving the room.

For a moment, there was nothing but silence as I studied my visitor. Could this be the same woman? The figure, hair, and features were all identical, but her countenance was completely different. She actually looked much younger. Her identity was undeniable, however, by the blouse she was wearing. It was the very one I had gotten her for Christmas. There was no mistake; I was sitting beside Gloria Stanton.

"Forgive me for coming without an invitation, Julia," she began, apologetically. "Because I was so terrible to you when David brought you home to meet us, I didn't want to call and ask to see you. I was afraid you might think I was looking for another opportunity to hurt you. But after seeing me, I hope you'll be more at ease and allow me to explain why my attitude toward you has completely changed. May I at least try?"

My heart was beating madly at the prospect of reconciliation with David's mother. "Of course," I answered. "I would like that."

Appearing happy and relieved, she suggested, "Why not pour our tea first, dear. I take mine black." I did as she requested, hoping my hands wouldn't shake, revealing how nervous I was.

After taking a few sips from her cup, Gloria smiled at me. "I suppose I should begin with the morning you and David left Baymont to return to Weston. Once you had gone, Bill came directly to our room and insisted we have a talk. He told me sternly things were going to change, that our time for grieving our loss of Carrie was over. I was shocked at his words. At my request, we never discussed our daughter's death, and in all our years of marriage, my husband had never talked to me so sharply.

"He went on to say, 'When our beautiful Carrie died, she gained heaven; she's enjoying the presence of God and much more than we could ever give her in this life, Gloria. But she was not our only child. You have a son who needs your love and support right now. I feel like David and I lost more than Carrie when she died; we lost *you*, Gloria! You are no longer the kind and caring woman I married. In fact, I don't even know you anymore.'

"I was furious he would say such a thing and told him so with shouts and accusations. Then I released my usual stream of tears, hoping to gain back my advantage over him. But he was no longer moved by such tricks. He walked into our bathroom and returned with a box filled with my medications. Placing them in front of me, he announced, 'I'm going to see the day when you're no longer taking *any* of these drugs. One by one, you're coming off these pills. It won't happen overnight or without professional help, but it will happen. I want my wife back!'

"When he said that, Julia, I knew he meant business, and panic gripped me. I couldn't imagine living without the help of those prescriptions. I was depending on them instead of God to get me through each day.

"Like many drug addicts, for that's exactly what I was, I was in denial. I refused to admit to myself that I had a problem. In my mind, nothing was *my* fault. Everyone was against me; nobody understood my needs or what I was going through. Enraged, I snatched the box from him and locked myself in the bathroom to sulk.

"Once the holidays were over, Bill located a facility where I could begin treatment. Woodland Meadows is a private treatment center about an hour from Baymont. It came highly recommended, and they could admit me immediately.

"When I found out what he was planning, I was furious. 'No one is going to put *me* in an institution!' I cried. 'What would my friends think? How could I ever show my face at the country club again? There is nothing wrong with me!' I insisted.

"I tried everything I could think of to play on his sympathies and get him to relent: crying fits, threats, and endless begging. Bill witnessed my antics stone-faced. When I saw that none of my pleading would change his mind, I bitterly shouted, 'All right, you win! I'll go. But don't expect me to cooperate with anyone at that place.'

"As you might imagine, my first weeks at the Meadows were quite miserable. Not because of the facility or medical staff; both were state of the art. I was the problem. There is no easy way to come off chemical dependency. While my prescriptions were slowly being replaced with live food, exercise, and natural remedies, I was going through all the normal pains of withdrawal.

"Because I was behaving so badly at the time, my husband asked David to drive to the Meadows and try to talk some sense into me. When he arrived, I railed on him as well. As delusional as I was then, I can still remember much of our conversation. When he tried to reason with me about cooperating with my treatment, I immediately turned on him about getting engaged to you instead of Cynthia.

"For several moments, he said nothing, his head down. At last, he raised his gaze. The look I received from my son instantly silenced me. I had never seen David look at me that way before. Soberly, he said, 'Mother, I will love you as long as you live, but I'm a grown man, and I will not allow you to run my life.

"'As it stands now, because you won't accept Julia into your heart or our family, she has refused to marry me. I love her, Mother! She's everything I want in a wife. She sincerely loves me, is devoted to God, and is the most caring woman I've ever known. So your objection to Julia isn't about Julia. It isn't that she has serious issues in her life and you're objecting to our marriage out of *tough love* to protect me. You object to Julia only because you want me to marry Cynthia.

"'So let me make something clear to you here and now: I will *never* marry Cynthia. That's *your* dream, not mine. I don't love her as anything more than a sister, and she's already in love with someone else!

"'I'm still trusting God that you will come to your senses so Julia and I can be together. Stop and think: if she doesn't marry me because of you, do you honestly believe I will *ever* feel the same toward you again? You already lost a child to cancer and now you're in danger of losing your son's respect and affection.

"'As a Christian, I am expected to honor you throughout my life. But it will be *your* choice whether I do it only out of obligation. I want to get married and live the life that God has for me. Why should I miss out on God's best because of your self-centeredness?

"'Mother, if you love me, really love me, you will let this obsession about Cynthia go and embrace the woman I truly love, trusting me to make the right decisions for my life.

"'As far as your stay here at the Meadows is concerned, either cooperate with your doctor and get well, or refuse his help and stay sick. Dad and I desperately want you to get better, to get your life back so we can be a whole family again, but we can't make that happen. It's entirely up to you. Try to remember that all our lives will be affected by your decision. I pray you make the right one.'

"Finished with what he came to say, he calmly walked over to my bed, kissed me goodbye, and left my room without looking back. David's words didn't have the full impact then that they would have later when I was recovered enough to actually feel concern for someone besides myself.

"I'm ashamed to think of how hateful I was to my doctor and his staff during my first weeks at the

Meadows. Bill visited me whenever he could, but his business affairs kept him away during the week. Isolation from my husband and friends worked toward my healing, though. The solitude gave me time for reflection and a lot of reading.

"I had been a Christian most of my life, Julia, but in later years, even before Carrie died, I'd gotten away from praying and reading the Bible. I'd accepted Jesus as my Savior, but I'd never made Him the Lord of my life. Truthfully, I had never felt the need."

Except for an occasional nod of acknowledgement here and there, I didn't interrupt Gloria from her story. I wanted to hear what she had to say as much as she wanted to tell me. So I listened intently as she went on.

"I grew up wealthy and spoiled with my father indulging my every whim, never wanting for anything. I was a fun, well-meaning person, but a bit of a snob who *did* want things her way. After graduating from college, I met Bill, and we were married a year later. I went from having a wealthy father to having a wealthy banker husband, a seamless transition in my fairy-tale life."

Gloria momentarily paused, reached for the teapot, and filled her cup. Settling back into a comfortable position, she took a few sips of her tea and then continued. "Now, back to my stay at the Meadows. As I was being weaned one by one from the drugs I'd been taking, my mind slowly returned to a more rational state, helping my attitude to improve toward those who were trying to help me—including my husband when he came to visit. My appetite increased, and I started to feel more like myself than I had in years.

"I had also started reading my Bible during those weeks," she stated, her face brightening. "The more Scripture I read, Julia, the more I wanted to read. In those verses, God seemed to be speaking to my heart in a way I'd never experienced before. Psalm 20:7 jumped out at me: 'Some trust in chariots and some in horses, but we trust in the name of the LORD our God.'

"The first half of that verse described me perfectly: I had grown up trusting in money and social power, not in the Lord. Truthfully, I had never related to God as much more than my ticket to heaven. I certainly didn't talk to Him, try to obey Him, or trust Him to take care of me. I thought myself capable of handling anything that came along. It took a devastating loss and confinement in a treatment center to convince me otherwise. People thought it was grief alone that drove me to drugs. But there was another reason behind my addiction, one that had been haunting me for years."

Gloria's Secret

I couldn't imagine what Gloria was about to tell me. I had to bite my lip to keep from asking what had haunted her so long. I didn't want to be rude, and Gloria's secret was hers to share in her own time. Even so, it was hard to be patient as she stopped to pour herself another cup of tea.

"I hope I'm not boring you with this rather detailed account," she said, turning to me again.

"Not at all," I assured her. "I couldn't be more interested. Please go on."

"Thank you, dear. My story really does have a purpose. Anyway, as I said before, I had enjoyed a fairy-tale life: a beautiful home, a loving husband, and two wonderful children. Then my perfect world was shattered when our twenty-one-year-old daughter was diagnosed with cancer.

"Julia, I don't think anyone can hear that news without being overtaken by disbelief and fear. Our initial reaction was that it had to be a mistake. Unfortunately, it wasn't. Additional tests proved her condition to be more advanced than originally thought. Carrie had to come home from college, and in the months to follow, we sought out the best-known cancer specialists using the latest medications and methods. Nothing we tried worked. All we could do was stand by helplessly and watch our daughter get progressively worse until she passed away.

"I responded to her death with anger and bitterness, blaming God for the loss of my daughter. As the weeks passed, my mind became so tormented, I couldn't sleep at night. My doctor gave me a prescription for sleeping pills, and that was the beginning of my drug-dependent history. More and more medications were added to help me cope with my grief and to offset the many side affects I was experiencing. Although the drugs helped to numb me, they couldn't treat the underlying reason for my torment—guilt."

Seeing her eyes fill with tears, I instinctively reached over, putting my hand on her shoulder to comfort her. "Carrie's illness wasn't your fault."

"No, Julia, but I felt responsible for making a serious error regarding her treatment. I've kept my mistake hidden for years, afraid and ashamed to tell anyone, especially Bill. Now both he and David know, and I want to tell you as well.

"Several months into Carrie's treatments, Bill and I could see she wasn't responding to the doctors' program for her, yet there seemed nothing more we could do except follow their treatment plan and hope she would begin to respond. Then one day I met a woman whose sister had survived cancer. She recommended a doctor named Feinberg, saying he had great success with even difficult cases. As she passed me a brochure, my heart swelled with hope at the prospect of having another expert look at Carrie. I tucked it in my purse to read later.

"When I got home and examined the brochure more closely, I saw that Dr. Feinberg used primarily natural methods. I thought, 'Natural methods? Is that even credible? We have no time to waste taking Carrie to someone like this. Besides, what would my friends think?' Then without even discussing it with Bill, I tossed the brochure into the trash. Six weeks later, our daughter died.

"I had completely forgotten the name Feinberg until David came home raving about some seminar speaker he had heard. He told me this doctor had great success with cancer patients and relayed the touching testimonies given by survivors that night, particularly one from a young woman who'd survived the same cancer that had taken Carrie's life.

"As I listened, I fought bitter thoughts at hearing this young woman survived, but Carrie didn't. When David said the doctor's name was Neil Feinberg, suddenly a terrible realization came over me. That was the doctor's name on the brochure I had thrown away! Immediately, remorse flooded my heart. Why had I acted so impulsively? Had I taken Carrie to this doctor, would she still be alive? I couldn't allow myself to consider such a possibility. The guilt would've been unbearable. So I refused to believe any of the claims made that night. I assured myself it was all a hoax, that my son was being deceived.

"Later, when I found out David planned to leave Baymont and join Dr. Feinberg's medical group, I was beside myself. No news could have been more upsetting to me. Now I would be constantly reminded that perhaps Carrie could've been helped had I swallowed my pride and taken her to this doctor for treatment. Though I had never met Dr. Feinberg, I hated him. The very mention of his name incensed me; I was willing to do anything to change my son's decision to study under him.

"David and Cynthia had spent a lot of time together after Carrie's death, talking and exercising the horses. I convinced myself they were a perfect match. Cynthia became the anchor I desperately needed to keep David in Baymont and away from Dr. Feinberg.

"When my son left to work in Weston, I continued to hold on to my hope that a marriage to Cynthia would draw David back home to me. Then you came along, Julia, threatening to ruin everything. When I heard of your engagement to David, I was determined to find a way to come between you. As you know all too well, I was successful.

"Even after I was making progress at the Meadows and reading my Bible again, I felt no regret for being the cause of your breakup with my son. My obsession to see him married to Cynthia was still very much alive—until she came to visit me a month ago and said she had recently married. She told me her husband owned several antique shops in Europe as well as the States, that they had met over a year ago while she was on a buying trip in Paris.

"After Cynthia left, I cried bitterly. All hope of David returning to Baymont was gone. There remained no way to avoid hearing the name Feinberg for the rest of my life or listening to David talk about those he had helped to survive cancer. I finally had to face the possibility that my daughter may have died because of my closed mind and senseless pride.

"I was off all but one of my medications by then, and my doctor had scheduled me to go home in a few short weeks. I was terrified. How was I going to deal with the pain of my guilt without drugs or a place like the Meadows to hide?

"That night I got little sleep. In the morning, I opened my Bible in search of comfort. Starting in the book of John, I kept reading until I reached John 8:32: 'Then you will know the truth, and the truth will set you free.'

"I repeated to myself over and over, *the truth will set you free.* Eventually, I realized God was speaking to me in that short phrase. He was telling me that I would never be free of my guilt about Carrie until I told the truth and confessed to someone what I had done. I wanted to obey Him, but I was ashamed to tell Bill or David. Because I had come to respect my doctor at the Meadows, he was the only one I felt ready to tell. As a fellow Christian, maybe he would have the perspective I needed.

"That afternoon, my doctor listened to my story patiently. His response brought such healing to me: 'Without seeing Carrie's medical history, there's no way for me to know how far advanced her cancer was when you heard about Dr. Feinberg. Since she died not long after that, she may not have responded to his treatment at that late date. The natural methods he incorporates into his practice are not miracle cures; they work gradually. Only God can do miracles. Dr. Feinberg and others like him merely use what God has given to us in nature that is known to help the body rebuild and repair.

"'All doctors lose patients, Gloria. None of us understands everything or has a perfect record. You and Bill did everything you knew to do for Carrie. Her suffering is over, and now that she's in heaven, it's time for you to stop blaming God and yourself for her death and start living life, free from both drugs and guilt. It's okay to forgive, be forgiven, and live again. Life can even be good once more if you'll let it.'

"With those words, years of oppression left me, and I felt like a new person. For the first time since Carrie's death, I was hopeful again. That day, I sincerely asked God to forgive me for blaming Him for Carrie's death, for living such a shallow Christian life, and for causing my family such pain. Then I chose to forgive myself, certainly the hardest part.

"I waited until Bill came to see me that weekend to tell him all that had happened. He freely forgave me, crying at the change he saw in me. All I could think of then was talking to David, but not on the phone. What I needed to say had to be done in person.

"Time dragged until I was finally released from the Meadows. I was anxious to see David right away, but Bill insisted that I settle in at home for a couple of days before leaving for Weston. I knew David had been told about my physical progress, but I wanted him to actually *see* the change in me before I asked for his forgiveness.

"During our time at home together, my husband shared with me how much I owe my recovery to *you*, Julia. He said that many of the things you said to him and David made them realize how seriously ill I was and encouraged them to finally stand up to me and make decisions in my best interest—decisions I wasn't able to make for myself. He told me how you and your whole family have been praying for me to get well all these months, even though I was the reason for your breakup with David.

"I did go to David today and ask his forgiveness for what I had done, all I had become. I'll always treasure what he said to me, the way he forgave me for the pain I'd caused. And now there is just one more person from whom I must ask forgiveness…

"Julia, can you ever forgive me for the horrible things I said and did to you when you stayed with us? I can only imagine how I hurt you with my heartless words. Please forgive me for the pain I've caused you, being separated from David for so long. I really don't know what to say other than I hope you understand me a little better now, and I'm so very sorry for it all."

My eyes welling up, I responded, "Of course, I forgive you, Gloria. And I'm so incredibly happy to see this new beginning for you. It makes everything we've gone through worth it."

Shedding tears of her own, Gloria gave me a grateful hug. "Thank you, Julia, I humbly accept your forgiveness. Now that I'm in my right mind again, I can see you're the perfect girl for our son. With all my heart, I want you and David to go ahead with your plans to be married. I promise I will love you as my very own daughter and I will never again interfere in your lives."

Overcome with emotion, I couldn't talk. Gloria opened her purse and handed me a handkerchief. As I took it from her and dabbed my wet cheeks, she said, "The time for tears is over, my dear, for all of us. So dry your eyes. Someone is anxiously waiting to hear from you. I made David promise he wouldn't come over until we'd had our talk. Here's my cell," she added, passing her phone to me. "I'm sure you know his number."

"By heart, thank you," I said, gratefully taking the phone from her. I was so excited, my fingers couldn't enter the numbers in fast enough. Once I finally managed to complete the call, it rang several times with no answer.

Just then, the doorbell rang. Looking over my shoulder, I saw my mom crossing the foyer to answer the door. She greeted someone and then gestured to the living room. David breezed right past my mom, and in a matter of seconds, I was in his arms. Picking me up with a twirl, he gave me a sensational kiss right in front of our mothers. When our lips parted, he looked at them and apologized. "Sorry! I've been storing up that kiss for over five months, and I couldn't hold it back anymore."

Gloria's reaction was a one-eighty from the last time she saw her son kiss me; this time she was delighted. In fact, she had her arm around my mom's shoulder, and they were both smiling from ear to ear.

Turning to Gloria, David remarked, "I know I promised not to come here until after you'd talked to Julia, but when an hour passed and I still hadn't gotten the okay, I decided to drive over and wait out front. But I just couldn't wait any longer."

Everyone laughed.

Then Gloria asked, "Where's your father?"

"Right here," my dad announced, escorting Bill into the living room. "It seems David left this poor man sitting all alone outside. When I pulled in the driveway just now and saw him in David's car, I decided to actually invite him in!"

Again everyone laughed, celebrating the extreme happiness of the moment. Introductions followed that hadn't been previously made between David's parents and mine. When they were over, Gloria reminded David, "I believe you have something that belongs to Julia, son. Don't you think you ought to return it?"

Turning toward me, David smiled, reached into his pocket, and pulled out my engagement ring. Taking my hand, he slipped it on my ring finger. "This time it's for keeps," he said before sealing his promise with another kiss.

"Looks like the Duncan family has a wedding to plan," Gloria commented, beaming. "Don't worry, I know the job of the mother of the groom: *shut up, show up, and wear beige.* That's a nice way of saying *stay out of the way.* This I'm determined to do. However, Bill and I would like to fulfill the traditional role of the groom's parents by paying for the flowers and rehearsal dinner, if you will allow us that privilege."

My dad noticed David and I were barely listening. We couldn't take our eyes off each other after being apart for so long. "It appears these young people would like some privacy. Let's adjourn to the kitchen where the rest of us can get better acquainted."

With that, the four parents left the room. Once they were gone, David seized the moment and kissed me again. "I just can't seem to get enough," he admitted, smiling.

I knew exactly how he felt. I certainly wasn't complaining. When he started to pull me down on the couch next to him, I resisted. "I've got a better idea. Let's go out back and sit on the swing where we can really be alone and talk."

To avoid any further conversation with our parents, we left by the front door and meandered down the curved walkway that led out back.

Chapter 21

Heart-to-Heart Talk

I t was almost seven when we rounded the corner to the backyard. The fountain in the center of my mother's flower garden bubbled peacefully as we passed it, making our way to the large platform swing placed under a tall maple tree on the far end of the lawn. Once we were seated side by side, David put his arm around me, pulled me close, and tenderly kissed my forehead.

"It's like a dream, Julia, being here with you like this," he said as we both pushed with our feet to put the swing in motion. "I've missed you so much. These last five months have been torture. There wasn't a moment you weren't in my thoughts."

"It was the same for me," I responded, comfortably resting my head on his shoulder. "I longed for you no matter where I went or what I did. I had to fight the fear that it might be years before we'd be together again."

"I fought those fears, too. Then I got a call this morning from my dad, saying he and my mother were coming to Weston. I knew she had been released from the Meadows a few days ago, but I was surprised that she'd want to travel here. I wasn't sure what to expect. My dad assured me I'd want to talk with them, that there was an important reason for their visit, so I agreed to meet them at my condo around four o'clock, right after I finished my rounds at the hospital. They got there ahead of me, and I found them waiting out front. When we met at the door, I couldn't believe the change in my mother."

"I know what you mean. She looks like a different person now. Did you see she's wearing the blouse I gave her?"

"I noticed it once we were inside my condo. It gave me hope that not only was she better physically, but maybe she'd had a change of heart about you as well.

"My dad wanted to see the rest of my place before we sat down on the couch to talk. Then my mother told me her whole story. We had a great moment together, and I forgave her completely. It was amazing to see my mom like this again, back to herself, but better, actually. When we were done talking, my parents had to practically hold me down to keep me from racing over here to give you the good news. My mom begged me to wait until she could talk to you first.

"Reluctantly, I agreed and gave her directions to your house. Before she left, I called to make sure someone would be home. When your mom answered, I told her my mother wanted to drive over and talk to you. She said you weren't home from work yet, that she expected you soon. I explained to her why my mother was coming, and she said to send her over right away."

"And now here we are together at last," I sighed, contentedly.

"Thank you so much, Julia."

"For what?"

"For your wisdom and courage—for challenging my dad and me to deal with my mother's problem. I don't know if God would've required every couple to handle this situation this way, but I know why God asked these months of separation from us."

"What do you mean?"

"Honestly, I needed to do some maturing before becoming a husband, Julia. While we were apart, I had a lot more time to read my Bible and pray. As I did, the Lord showed me that because I'd grown up watching my father appease, instead of confront my mother, I had become just like him, especially since Carrie died. As much as I hated to admit it, it wasn't so much about protecting my mother as it was about making things less complicated for my dad and me. It was easier not to deal with her issues, to just work around them. You picked up on that the first time we were with my parents."

"It wasn't hard to recognize, David."

"Maybe for you, but my dad and I sure didn't see it until you pointed it out. I went along with our breakup *only* because that's what you and your parents felt we should do. It wasn't what I wanted. I would've been willing to marry you without my mother's blessing."

"David, I hope you know how hard it was for me to say *no* when I wanted to marry you with all my heart."

"As hard as it was on both of us, you made the right decision. Truthfully, had you agreed to marry me in spite of my mother's objections, I'm not sure how well I would've shielded you from her. Maybe I would have in the beginning, but as time went on, I probably would've slipped back into my old habit of just ignoring her bad behavior, trying to downplay the hateful things she said and did to you. It's easy to think you're fair and objective when you're not the one being hurt.

"Your dad was right: Even though I was angry with my mother for the way she was acting, I really love her. I would've been in the middle, trying to do the impossible, to keep the two women I loved happy.

"I probably would've asked you to be the better person and put up with her nonsense until she changed. It's funny; if it were anyone else trying to hurt you, I'd defend you with my life. But somehow it was different with my mother; I made excuses for her. It took being without you this long to make me see you are, without question, the most important person in my life."

"David, that means so much! Every woman wants the man she loves to put her needs and feelings ahead of everyone else's. If she knows she's number one with her husband, she'll follow him to the ends of the earth."

"Well, you're definitely number one with me—and you always will be."

David drew me in close and kissed me before saying, "Thanks for staying in faith all these months, Julia, for doing what you felt God wanted, for not putting your love for me ahead of your love for God."

"He gave me the grace to do it, I guess. I had waited for you for so long; all my dreams were finally coming true. It would have been easy for me to ignore your mom's threats and simply hope things would work out better after we were married. Only I know better than that. I've seen too many marriages crumble because of in-law problems.

"I had to think beyond my love for you and consider our children and how my decision to marry you might affect their lives. Being madly in love today doesn't guarantee a happy, lasting marriage. No couple can know everything up front, but I at least knew for sure that I didn't want Gloria Stanton to be my mother-in-law *or* my children's grandmother. Not the way she was.

"That doesn't mean that while we were separated, I wasn't tempted to change my mind. I don't know how many times I picked up my phone, wanting to call the whole thing off. It was the Lord who kept me strong. In my heart, I was confident that if He really meant for us to be together, He would find a way to turn your mother's feelings for me around. And He did!"

"Julia, my mother wouldn't be well today if you hadn't listened to God. I know her new relationship with Him will make her a better, happier person than she was even before losing Carrie."

"Well, Jesus always makes that difference in a yielded heart, right? Your mom not only found freedom from her guilt and grief; she discovered her Lord."

"Let's get married right away," David blurted out, unexpectedly.

I couldn't help laughing because he looked at me so anxiously, as though tomorrow wouldn't be soon enough. Smiling, I leaned my head back against his chest. "Let's not rush things, David. I have one term left this fall before getting my master's. Once school's over, I'll have more time to plan the perfect wedding for us. We can look at our calendars soon and pick a date, but for now, all I want is to be close to you like this and enjoy this moment together."

"Okay, let's thank the One who made it possible."

I nodded my agreement. For the next several minutes, we prayed together, thanking God for making a way for our love to be realized. Until that afternoon, it had seemed beyond our reach.

It was almost dark before we finished our heart-to-heart talk on the swing and headed back into the house. Our parents had already eaten something, but not wanting to disturb us, they hadn't called us to the table. We joined them at the breakfast nook. By then, David and I were both hungry. My mom quickly heated up two plates she had already set aside for us.

While we were eating, we had a great time visiting with our parents. This was something I had never expected to see: Gloria Stanton, sitting at a simple kitchen table, completely at ease and having a wonderful time. It was obvious by Bill's frequent smiles that he was grateful to have his wife back.

David's parents stayed for the rest of the weekend. My mom invited them to be our guests while they were in Weston, but they had already checked into a hotel by David's condo. However, they accepted a dinner invitation for the next night. Kitty prepared a delicious meal that was served in our formal dining room. It wasn't the impressive spread I'd had at the Stantons' home, but it was perfect all the same.

All evening, David's parents appeared to enjoy themselves. My dad and Bill were like-minded in business matters, and my mother and Gloria found many things to talk about together. David and I were thrilled to see our parents relating so well. We felt like pinching each other to make sure this was real and not a dream. Just two days ago, this scenario had seemed impossible!

Bill and Gloria met the rest of my relatives at church the next morning. After service, John's family and my grandparents joined us for a meal at our house. My mom was the usual gracious hostess, and I was proud of her. I hoped to be the same someday, when the house was David's and mine. How I loved the sound of that!

Before going home to Baymont that evening, Bill announced that he and Gloria were leaving the following week on an extended European tour—sort of a second honeymoon. Meanwhile, our wedding plans had gotten as far as booking the Weston Inn for our reception the following August.

For the rest of the summer, David and I spent every free moment playing in the sun and spending evenings together on the swing out back. Once, when we were kissing, David abruptly pulled away and got off the swing, walking a few paces away. When I looked at him questioningly, he smiled and assured me, "Nothing's wrong, Julia. I just need a break. That last kiss was all a godly man can take and still act godly."

Suddenly, I remembered something John had confessed to me years before—that after spending evenings on that same swing with Jenny during their courtship, he would have to put on his tennis shoes and run off his sexual frustrations. Recalling his story reminded me to be more sensitive to what David was going through physically as he attempted to keep his passion for me under control until we were married. I loved receiving his kisses, but I wasn't fighting the same temptations he was. From then on, at my suggestion, we tried to spend less time alone and limited our kissing as much as a couple in love can be expected to do.

Once my fall classes started up, David and I didn't have as much time to be together. I had been right to anticipate a demanding schedule. I was so pressed for time, another leader had to take over my girls' group at church for a while.

Finishing my schooling felt like climbing a mountain: The closer I got to the top, the more effort I had to exert to get there. But once I finally reached the summit, my final semester completed, I was elated. All those hours of hard work were over; I had my master's degree at last! Now all I had to concentrate on was my job at the Center, getting ready for the holidays, and spending more time with the man I loved.

David's parents had been back from Europe for several months and were undergoing some major changes in their lives. Gloria wrote me all about it in a card she had sent for my graduation. She said she and Bill were selling their large estate and downsizing. With Carrie gone and David out of town, they no longer wanted to live in that big mansion or keep horses. Gloria was ready to let go of the past and build a new and better future with her husband.

Hearing of a young woman in Baymont who had lost her horse in an accident, Gloria invited the girl and her parents to come out and meet the horse that had belonged to Carrie. When Emma mounted Majesty, there was an instant bond. Watching them work out together, it was apparent that Emma was not only a lovely girl, but a talented equestrienne as well.

Confident she had found the match she wanted, Gloria asked Emma's parents for permission to gift the horse to their daughter. In Carrie's memory, the Stantons wanted to set up a fund to pay for Majesty's upkeep, Emma's riding lessons, and all tournament expenses.

Emma's parents were in shock at first, unable to comprehend receiving such a blessing. Gloria assured them they would be doing the Stantons a favor by accepting. When they told Emma, she laughed and cried at the same time; she couldn't stop thanking Gloria or hugging Majesty.

Gloria wrote, "Julia, never before had I experienced the true joy of having money. Nothing I'd ever donated to make myself look good had given me such deep satisfaction. Bill told me for years that money was a tool and not a trophy. Now I finally know what he meant."

As I read her letter, I was certain this was just the beginning of a lifetime of giving to others for David's mother. She had been a part of many charities in the past, but her motives for giving had not been pure. Now they were.

I was grateful that although David had been raised with money, it definitely was not his god. He had a generous and balanced heart, no doubt from his father. One day he would inherit the Stantons' wealth. I was glad to know that while my husband would have a great deal of money, money would never have him.

Reality Check

With school behind me, I could finally focus on planning the wedding of my dreams. It was so fun designing the perfect day with David and my mom! Gloria was true to her word. She didn't interfere with any of the details concerning the ceremony or reception. She offered her opinions only when asked, assuring us that it was our day and everything should be exactly as *we* wanted it. Knowing she would never have this moment with a daughter of her own, I tried to include her in lots of special ways.

Choosing the right gown became my biggest concern. I thumbed through every bridal magazine I could find, but still wasn't set on any one style. I only knew the dress would have to be magical, making me feel like a princess.

For three weekends in a row, my mom and I hit all the local bridal shops. I liked several gowns, yet none were exactly what I wanted. I wondered if I was being too picky, but my mother assured me I would know my dress the moment I put it on. I was skeptical, worried it was taking me too long to make up my mind.

The following Saturday, we went to a boutique tucked away in a small town thirty minutes from Weston. Certain she had just what I was looking for, the owner ushered my mother and me into a large dressing room.

Shortly, the lady returned with a long, zippered bag and hung it on a hook on the back of the door. As she removed the dress from the bag, my heart skipped a beat. This was by far the most elegant gown I'd seen.

The woman brought it over to me, holding it open so I could carefully step inside. Then she raised it up and proceeded to zip up the back. Standing on the raised platform, I looked into the three-way mirror in front of me. I actually gasped when I saw myself. Never before had I felt so beautiful—like a modern day Cinderella.

My mother had been right, as usual. This was *my* dress, exactly what I'd hoped to find. Studying my reflection from every angle, I couldn't stop smiling. Happy and relieved, the rest of the time was spent trying on veils until I found just what I had envisioned.

Seeing how perfect my gown and veil looked together, my heart was bursting with gratitude. God had been so faithful to me! My day had finally come! Soon I would marry the man for whom I had invested years of patience and sacrifice. Having someone like David to love for a lifetime made the struggle seem small in comparison. He was my Mr. Right, and I was the girl he had forsaken all others to wait for and marry.

We asked Cassie and Brian to be our matron of honor and best man. David chose Brian because they'd become close friends during our five-month breakup. Brian knew how much David missed me and stood by him when he was down and needed encouragement. We asked Jenny, John, Melody, and Flip to be the rest of our bridal party. Of course, Magda would be our flower girl and eighteen-month-old John Jr., our ring bearer.

When it was time to order our flowers, I called Gloria to see if she could come into town to help me. She was excited I had asked her, saying she'd come alone to Weston for the weekend since Bill was away on business.

My mom offered her our guest room, and much to my surprise, Gloria accepted the invitation. David's mother and I had been developing a closer relationship by emailing and talking on the phone occasionally, yet I was still a little nervous about having her stay with us. Because of her past criticisms of me, I was still keeping my guard up. Rebuilding trust in a relationship takes time.

My secret fears were put to rest because that weekend with David's mother went fabulously. She arrived on Friday evening around dinnertime, ate with my parents, and spent the evening with them. David and I were attending a benefit dinner for the hospital that night.

The following morning when I went downstairs, I found both our mothers in the kitchen, finishing breakfast. They were laughing about something as I came into the room.

"What's so funny?" I inquired, pouring myself a tall glass of orange juice.

"Just trading college experiences," Gloria replied from where she was seated with my mother at the breakfast nook. "Your mom told me *you* had quite an experience with one of your professors after meeting David, that my son had to rescue you from him at the hospital that first night. Grace won't tell me anything else. I've been waiting for you to come down so I can hear the whole story. Please don't keep me in suspense. What happened?"

Getting a muffin and some scrambled eggs from the stove, I joined them at the table. Between mouthfuls, I related the whole McNulty nightmare, how David had saved me in the nick of time. Then Gloria wanted to know all about our early courtship and how David and I had fallen in love. She laughed when I shared about the time I thought Sandy was another girl David was seeing.

The rest of the morning was spent getting ready to leave for lunch and then the florist. Gloria invited my mother to join us for the day. She wanted to eat at the country club so she could see the dining room and talk to the manager about having our rehearsal dinner there. After lunch, she booked the facility for the Friday night before our wedding. Then we all left for Lyndall's.

So many choices! I had no idea picking out flowers would be this involved. A bit overwhelmed, I was glad my mom and Gloria were there to make some helpful suggestions. After what seemed like hours of looking through books of different arrangements, I finally made all my decisions, including my selection for the bridal bouquet. Much to the surprise of both mothers, I decided on daisies. They were the first flower David had sent me, and my favorite as well. He had sent those first daisies to thank me for being his best friend. Since I was marrying my best friend for life, I thought they were a perfect choice.

That evening after dinner, we had a girls' night in with popcorn and a romantic comedy. It was an older film, and all three of us laughed until our sides ached. When the movie was over, Gloria turned to my mom and me. "I can't begin to tell you what this weekend has meant. Thank you for including me in all of this. I haven't had moments like these in years."

Instantly, I was reminded how special it was to have my mom as a close friend, to be able to have fun with her like this. I was grateful to be able to have fun with Gloria, too. I knew it had been tragic for her to lose her only daughter, but I'd never thought of it in this context before, missing out on all the *girl times* together.

The next day, Gloria planned to leave for Baymont right after church. David and I walked her to her car following the service. Once David had kissed her goodbye, she turned and gave me a hug, whispering in my ear, "It's wonderful to have a daughter again, Julia. Thank you." I could tell by the catch in her voice, she really meant it. Then she smiled at the two of us, got in her convertible, and drove off.

David didn't say anything, but I could tell from his expression he was happy to have a good relationship with his mother again after so many years—and that he was excited she and I were becoming close. I knew I could never replace Carrie, but I hoped I could continue to bring mother/daughter-in-law joy to Gloria's heart.

The following months evaporated into all the other decisions and preparations every bride must make before her special day. David and I discussed everything, but he left most of the final choices up to me, saying, "Whatever makes you happy makes me happy. The only thing I care about having is *you*."

The Stantons gave us a large amount of money as an early wedding gift, which we used to purchase land on the edge of Weston. We planned to start building a house once we got home from our honeymoon. Until the house was done, we'd start married life in David's condo.

Next we had to register for our shower gifts. David and I had fun picking out our linens, dishes, and kitchen things. We tried to stick to basic styles and colors that would fit into any décor we might choose for our future home.

We were humbled by the generosity of our family and friends at our shower. What a haul! We decided to store everything in the spare bedroom at David's condo until after the wedding. I wanted to wait until I was living there to put everything away.

Before I knew it, David was at his bachelor's party at John's place, and I was having my personal shower at Cassie's. When it was time to open my gifts, I experienced firsthand how Cassie and Melody must have felt at their showers. Opening box after box of alluring nightwear and lacy lingerie, I laughed good-naturedly and pretended to be unaffected by the teasing I was receiving. Inside, however, I was having a mild panic attack! It hit me that David would be seeing me in all this, that soon I'd be his wife and experiencing everything that went with it. What a reality check!

When my mom and I got home, we carried the gifts up to my room. Closing the door behind us, I walked over and pulled her down next to me on my bed for a mother-daughter chat.

"I'm starting to feel a little anxious, Mom," I confided. "All my life, I've had a mindset of *no sex*. But on my wedding night, what's always been taboo will suddenly be okay. How does a girl who has never had sex transition from withholding her body to freely giving it to her husband?"

My mom smiled at me. "God will help you make that transition, Julia. Try to remember that David is probably experiencing similar feelings."

"What if I disappoint him?"

"Don't worry about that, honey. Men find pleasure in sex the very first night. For women, lovemaking is often a learned art. Don't expect all fireworks in the beginning. It takes time for your body to adjust to receiving a man. You and David have the rest of your lives to discover how to please one another during your intimate times together. Just learn to be a good communicator. You're scared now because you're about to experience a whole new dimension of love with David. He's probably nervous himself about doing everything right. Do you still have the book I gave you?"

"Yes, it's in my desk. But you said not to read it yet."

"I wanted you to wait until you'd had your personal shower. Now that your wedding day is so close, it's time for you to read it. After you've finished, if you have any questions, I'll be here to answer them for you.

"Remember, Julia, God is the author of marital love, and what you're about to experience with David is a very natural, beautiful thing. It's something you'll share only with him for your lifetime together. It's incredibly wonderful and special. Because you've waited for each other, you have no regrets, wounds, or comparisons to deal with. There's no shame when sex is done the right way, Julia. It's something God wants you to value and enjoy, so instead of being afraid of your wedding night, look forward to it! It will be a memory you'll have forever."

I smiled, thinking about being able to make such a memory with a man like David. I silently thanked God for putting me with someone gentle and kind like him.

Instantly, another thought came to me. I felt I already knew the answer, but wanted my mom's input anyway. "What about girls who haven't waited? They can still have a great marriage, a beautiful wedding night, right?"

"That's a complex question, Julia. It would be hard for me to do it justice in just a few minutes here tonight. But let me simply say that God loves each of His daughters unconditionally. So if a girl has had sex before marriage, she can sincerely ask God to forgive her, and He will. But in order to enjoy a better future, she needs to realize that according to God's standards, sex outside of marriage is wrong. She will have to choose to make a lifestyle change and ask God to help her stay sexually pure from that point on. Once she's cooperating with God by following His biblical guidelines, she can have a beautiful wedding night and great marriage because God has forgiven her past mistakes and shown her a new and better way to live."

As I listened to my mom, I was struck with how blessed I was to have someone with whom I could talk about anything and everything. I was grateful she always kept my conversations with her confidential, that whatever I shared with her was safe. My grandmother was the same way. I could be genuine with her and ask for real input in return. I always benefited from her many years of experience and godly wisdom.

A week before my personal shower, my grandmother had asked me out for lunch, just the two of us. Although David and I were finishing marriage counseling sessions with our pastor, I was anxious to talk with my grandma to get any advice she might have for me.

I picked up my grandma at noon, and we drove to a quaint little French café downtown. We asked to be seated outside, and as we sat beneath the shelter of a large overhead umbrella, enjoying our food, we talked about a lot of valuable things for starting my new life with David.

One of the things she shared was that according to Scripture, becoming David's wife meant entering into a covenant with him, becoming one with him—not just sexually, but one in purpose and destiny. His call would become my call, his mission, my mission; we would learn to be two people functioning as one. She warned me that a married woman must not have dreams and ambitions that interfer with her responsibilities as a wife and mother.

She clarified that statement by saying, "That doesn't mean God expects you to waste your gifts and talents or give up your personal dreams, Julia. It only means those things will need to be woven into the fabric of your marriage in a balanced way and expressed through the many seasons of your life.

"You'll find that each season offers different freedoms and restrictions. Before children arrive, you and David will both have time for many things: uninterrupted intimacy, careers, and lots of recreational time together. But after the birth of a child, you'll move into a different season: raising a precious life! You must keep your marriage vibrant and healthy, a major priority still, but your lifestyle will need to adjust to accommodate a child's needs.

"Always remember what a huge responsibility it is to raise children, Julia. Those beautiful little ones are eternal souls; their understanding of God, sense of worth, and character development depend greatly on you and David and what you invest in them when they are young. Savor the years you have with your children, Julia. They are priceless!

"One day, it will be just you and David again, and things will shift in a new way. Throughout your life, God will help you realize your dreams as you listen to His direction, keep your husband and family as your top priority, and live life fully.

"Be careful to enjoy each season you're in at the time, Julia. You don't want to miss any of its joy wishing for the past or longing for the future. Let each current season be beautiful and satisfying. Then one day, you'll look back and thank God for a truly fulfilling life."

After that talk with my grandmother, I decided I needed to spend some time alone before the wedding.

I wanted to read through my journals and review my journey to this place of marriage, the place I had believed to reach for so long. I wanted to take some extended time to thank God for His faithfulness, and to meditate on the changes I would undergo in this new season of life.

I had once heard that in ancient Jewish wedding customs, a woman was baptized before getting married. Being lowered beneath the water symbolized her decision to *leave behind* her former life as a single woman; being raised up out of the water signified her willingness to take up her role as a married woman, recognizing all the dynamics involved.

David didn't fully understand why I wanted to spend a few days alone at the cottage right before our wedding, but he supported my going as long as I took Sandy for some added protection. I promised to call him as soon as I got back.

The last time I saw David was when he kissed me goodbye before I left for the cottage on Sunday afternoon. I could still feel the warmth of his lips on mine.

Suddenly, my mind was no longer reviewing past events; my full attention returned to my car where I was helplessly trapped on a deserted country road. The rest of my story with David would be lived once I was found and rescued.

And I *was* going to be rescued! I just had to be. Sighing, I began to pray again: *Lord, I trust You to get me to my wedding Saturday! I'm believing that I will walk down the aisle to David in my beautiful wedding dress—the one that's hanging in the corner of my room, waiting for me to put on. I'm trusting that everything will still go as planned; this crazy accident will not spoil a thing! Please help me to continue to believe...*

It's dark now, and I have no idea what time it is. The moon must be full because even though it's incredibly foggy, a glow is still filtering in through the tree overhead. Thank You for not leaving me in total darkness. I was so hoping not to be here tonight, Lord. But still, I know You have a plan.

I thought nighttime would bring cooler air into this stuffy car, Father! I'm surprised how hot and humid it still is, even without the sun. At least I've been sweating so much all day, my bladder doesn't feel uncomfortably full. If possible, let me be found before I have to do something about it! And please help my back; it's getting stiff sitting in this position for so long. I still can't pull my legs free, and I don't know how much longer I can stand being trapped like this!

I really want this to be over, Lord. Help me! Please get me out of here. I'm going to close my eyes and try to sleep now. In Jesus' name, watch over me through the night, and let David and my family find me soon. Please, God...

Chapter 23

Blessing in Disguise

I awoke the next morning, still in my car, still lost.
I knew that help needed to come soon. I was out
of food and water and still couldn't budge under the
steering wheel. Nothing seemed to be broken, but it
couldn't be good for my circulation to be pinned for
this long.

I had been confined in my car for almost twenty-
four hours. Surely people were somewhere on the
road above, perhaps looking for survivors of the
storm. They might not be able to hear me if they were
driving by in their cars, but they might if they were
searching the area on foot. If I didn't start making
some noise right now, my chances were slim anyone
would know I was down here.

Hoping for a miracle, I pushed the horn again and
tried the radio, but they still weren't working. Just
then, I heard a car motor up above. Excited, I started

calling out for help, over and over until my vocal chords nearly gave out, yet there was no response. Whoever it was, they hadn't stopped. Fighting back tears, I decided to rest my voice for a while in case I needed to scream later to get someone's attention.

How I wished I had some water for my dry throat! All that yelling had taken its toll, and I could feel how dehydrated I was getting.

Opening the console, I fished David's watch out of its gift box. Gently, I rubbed my thumb across the lid and prayed again that I would still be able to give it to him.

Flipping the watch open, I closed my eyes. As I listened to the tin melody playing, I pictured David searching for me, finding me, holding me, telling me he loved me. The tune played over and over as I thought of David. His face. His smile. His kiss. The sound of his voice whispering my name...

Suddenly, I thought I heard David's voice, his *real* voice! Instantly, I screamed for help as tears began spilling down my cheeks. Despite my raw throat, I kept calling out his name until I heard him right above me.

"I hear you, Julia!" David shouted down. "Are you all right?"

"Yes, I think so. Only I'm pinned under the steering wheel. Please get me out of here, David!"

"Hold on a little longer, babe. We have a rescue team just a few minutes away."

I heard excited shouts above. Next my brother called down to me, telling me to hang in there; help was on the way. My dad's voice followed, assuring me they would get me out very soon. I was already crying, but hearing their voices released all the tears I had been holding back for hours and hours.

In a matter of minutes, I heard trucks, machines, and more shouting from people I loved—my mom, my grandpa, Jenny, and even Flip. Some rescue workers climbed down into the ravine, calling out instructions to me as they threaded a blanket through the branches. I was told to place it over my face and upper body to protect me from glass and flying sawdust. From under the blanket, I could hear the men sawing the tree branches covering my car into smaller pieces so they could be more easily taken away.

Once that was done, two of the men removed the shattered windshield and worked to cut through the steering wheel connection, freeing my legs at last. What an immense relief! Carefully pulling me out through the front windshield area, I was placed on a stretcher as a precaution until I could be examined for injuries. Then the rescue team carried the stretcher up the slope and passed it to David and John, where they had both been instructed to wait at the ledge. They pulled it over the edge and set it down gently. Dropping to his knees beside me, David didn't say a word. He just leaned down and held me close.

"I love you so much, Julia," he finally said, choking back tears as he stroked my hair. "Thank God we found you in time." The rest of my family couldn't wait any longer; they all crowded around me.

After everyone had a chance to say something to me, David did a preliminary check for broken bones and any damage to my spine. Confident I had no serious injuries, he carefully helped me from the stretcher and picked me up in his arms. Then I made an unexpected request.

"Put me down, David. I want to walk."

David shook his head. "Don't push it, Julia. We still need to check your vitals and make sure you're okay."

"I know, but I need to do this."

Reluctantly, David lowered me to my feet. A little wobbly at first and still holding on to David's arm, I managed to take several steps on my own. Smiling up at him, I said, "I believed I'd walk away from this accident, and now I have. God is so faithful!" Turning to my mother and Jenny, I cried, "Get me to a bathroom, quick!"

David picked me up again and carried me to the entrance of a motor home parked a few feet away. I recognized it as the one we kept up at the cottage. Once inside, I was guided by my mother to the bathroom. There I was able to finally relieve an almost bursting bladder.

When I came out, I shed my dirty clothes, washed up, and put on the fresh outfit that had been brought for me. Jenny checked my vital signs, announcing they were okay. Then she handed me a water to start hydrating again, and my mom gave me something to eat. As I devoured a sandwich, the men were invited in to see me. Sandy quickly pushed her way ahead of them and placed her head on my lap.

"So glad you made it, too, girl!" I said, gratefully hugging the dog.

My grandfather walked up and kissed me on the forehead. "I just called your grandmother with the good news, Julia. She sends her love and will call around to let people back home know you're all right."

Everyone was amazed I had come through my ordeal without any major injuries, nothing but a few surface scratches on my face from flying glass, some large bruises on my thighs, and a stiff back from sitting at an angle for so long.

David immediately called the chiropractor at Dr. Feinberg's office and set up a time to bring me in for an adjustment later that afternoon. "I can't have my bride leaning to one side during our wedding," he teased.

When my dad started up the motor home to head back to Weston, I asked if I could speak to Flip before we left. He was still outside working on getting my car out of the ravine. He was glad to have a chance to talk with me before I left for home.

"Do me a favor, will you, Flip?"

"Name it, Julia girl."

"My suitcase is in the trunk. Can you grab it once you get my car out and drop it off at my house later? My journals are in there; I don't want them to get lost. My keys are still in the ignition. I tried to use the radio, but my battery must be dead. The car's totaled, isn't it?"

"Yep, even I can't fix it. But cars can be replaced, ya know? I'm just glad *you* didn't get totaled," he said with a wink. Before stepping out the door, he turned back to me. "Actually, Julia, slidin' into the ravine when ya did was a good thing. Drivin' in that storm, ya wouldn't've seen that there's a bridge out a little ways down the road; ya would've driven right over the edge. Not sure ya could've survived *that* crash."

"Are you serious? I didn't know about the bridge! Wow, I guess my accident was a blessing in disguise. God put me in the safest place possible during that tornado. All I had to do was sit tight and trust Him to get me out somehow."

When the motor home finally pulled away from the scene, my parents were driving up front as David and I sat together in the back. John and Jenny were bringing some of the other vehicles home while my grandfather stayed behind with the men who were still working to get my car out.

On the drive back, I sat close to David, my head resting on his chest. I was anxious to hear how they had pieced together the details of my disappearance, how they had eventually found me. David shifted into a comfortable position himself and then explained:

We didn't find out you were missing until yesterday afternoon. Your mom got worried when you didn't call her back, so she and your dad called the Gordons at the cottage. When they didn't answer their cell, your dad called around and found out a severe storm and tornado had ripped through the Judson Falls area that morning. He tried the Gordons again and got through. Mrs. Gordon said the cottage hadn't suffered any serious damage.

When your mother asked to talk to you, Mrs. Gordon told her you had decided to leave a day ahead of schedule, that you had taken off after breakfast. She said you were on the road in plenty of time to miss the storm and had no idea why you hadn't made it back to Weston yet.

Thinking you might have stopped to see Cassie, Jenny, or your grandparents before coming home, your dad called them next. Nobody had seen or heard from you. It was late afternoon by that time; something was definitely wrong. You were clearly missing, but why?

Your dad called me at the hospital right away, hoping I'd heard from you. I hadn't, of course. When he told me what he suspected, I was worried out of my mind. I got someone to cover for me and left immediately.

When I got to your house, your dad had already gotten the family together. Your parents, Jenny and John, and your grandparents were sitting in the living room, waiting for me to arrive.

Scanning the room, everyone looked as baffled and scared as I was. Your grandfather led us in prayer, asking God to help us figure out what had happened. We had so little to go on.

While we were trying to figure out what to do next, my cell rang. It was a guy named Tony from a gas station in Judson Falls. He said he had Sandy there, that he was calling the number on her tag.

I asked if you were with her, but he knew nothing of you. When I told him you and Sandy were traveling together, he said he'd found glass particles in Sandy's fur. My heart sank when I heard that. I knew you must've been in an accident. Yet if Sandy was all right, I had to believe you were, too. She wouldn't have left you unless you had sent her out for help.

The realization that you must be hurt hit me hard. I envisioned you out there somewhere waiting to be found, needing help. But where were you and how badly were you injured? Were you still alive? I couldn't let myself think that way. You had to be alive. You had to be!

I needed more information. Something, anything that might help me find you. Shaking off my fears, I asked Tony where he had found Sandy. He said a man had brought her into the store, saying he'd found her on Woodland Road, that he wanted to drop her off somewhere safe. I asked Tony if he'd gotten the man's name. He said it was Damon something or other, that he was probably a hitchhiker because he was alone and wearing a backpack. Once Tony had agreed to take the dog, the man left right away. That's all Tony could tell me.

After hanging up, I relayed the conversation to your family. Nobody could figure out why you'd be anywhere near Woodland Road. The timing of all this was off as well. If you had left when Mrs. Gordon said, then why were you still in the area when the storm hit?

That's when your mom remembered you were going to swing by a jewelry store in Judson Falls before coming home. She said stopping there could've delayed you long enough to put you in the path of the storm.

I was frustrated that so much of this was still guesswork. Your dad said Woodland Road was a shortcut from Judson Falls to Weston, but it was such a rough road, he never used it. He didn't think you even knew about it. I concluded that someone must have told you about the shortcut, that you had taken it to make better time. Since that was where Sandy was found, we decided to start looking for you there.

Brian and Cassie watched the kids for John and Jenny so they could come with us to search for you. Within the hour, your dad and I left with John in his SUV for Judson Falls. Your mom and Jenny drove separately and headed for the cottage to pick up the motor home, thinking we might need it once we'd found you.

Your grandparents stayed behind to organize a local search and rescue crew. Flip was called right away. He and your grandpa started getting all the men and equipment needed to move debris and free your car, if necessary. They were to follow when they got everything together.

About 10 miles out of Judson Falls, John turned onto Woodland Road so we could look for your car. Driving was slow since it was already starting to get dark. The air was heavy with mist; it was hard to see much ahead. While your brother drove, your dad and I hung out the back windows, shining lights on either side of the road. There were fallen trees all over; John had to steer around some big ones blocking the way.

We noticed there was no oncoming traffic all this time and wondered why. We got our answer a few miles later when we pulled up to a frightening sight. Apparently, the tornado had touched down on the stretch of road just in front of us, destroying the bridge there. Sick to my stomach, I prayed we wouldn't find your car crashed in the river below.

Jumping out of the SUV, the three of us rushed to the edge and shined our lights down on the rushing water. From what we could tell, your car wasn't there. Relieved but shaken, we got back into the SUV. Your dad tried to stay positive, pointing out that this wasn't a waste; at least we knew where you weren't, that you must be on the other side of the bridge somewhere. His words made sense, but the silence in the car on the way to Judson Falls confirmed how worried all three of us were.

When we finally got there, we picked up Sandy at the gas station. Tony had called the guy working the morning shift and found out he had seen you that day and given you directions for the shortcut. So now we knew we were looking in the right area. We just had to search along the road on the other side of the bridge.

Before heading for Woodland Road, Tony suggested we stop by the town hall. With so much damage from the storm, officials had turned it into a temporary shelter and hospital. I didn't want to waste time, but I had to check to see if you were there. Maybe someone had found you already.

We looked in all the rooms for you, but you weren't anywhere. I asked if survivors had been found on Woodland Road, only to learn that rescue workers hadn't even gotten there yet. Less populated areas wouldn't be getting help for a while. We were anxious to keep searching, but one of the county officers at the shelter practically ordered us to hold off. A heavy fog had rolled in, making it impossible to see more than a few feet ahead. With all the debris on the road, it was too dangerous to chance a search. That meant we'd have to wait until the fog lifted, hopefully by morning.

Not knowing what else to do, we went back to the gas station and watched for the girls. They arrived in the motor home about thirty minutes later. We parked it in an open area and all found a place inside to rest and wait together.

I couldn't sleep, thinking of you all alone out there in the dark. Restless, I went back to John's

SUV and prayed. Hard. For hours. I couldn't accept that we were this close to our life together only to have it snatched away.

You're the girl I'd prayed for my whole life, Julia. God had brought us together that first night at the hospital, and then when we had to work through that mess with my mother, I had to trust Him to bring you back to me again. This was just one more time to trust His faithfulness.

By daylight, the fog had lifted, and your grandfather, Flip, and their crew had shown up as well. In their group were some volunteer firefighters from Weston, friends of Flip. They had brought some heavier equipment just in case it was needed.

With everyone grabbing some sandwiches your mom had packed, we all got into our vehicles and left for Woodland Road to start searching. When we arrived, we had to steer around a sign warning that the bridge was out. We had reported that to the police the night before; they must have posted that sign sometime during the night.

It was agreed that John, your dad, and I would scout ahead, calling back for help if we found your car. I brought Sandy with us, thinking we might need her to find you. The rest of the crew was inching along behind us, trying to make a more thorough search of the area.

Just like the night before, there was a lot of debris on the road, but it was easier maneuvering around it in the daytime. It was a longer stretch of road on this side of the bridge, and searching for you seemed to take forever. It was frustrating trying to cover so much area.

When we reached that same destroyed bridge, John stopped his SUV, and we jumped out to check the river below—this time in the daylight. Your car was nowhere in sight. Although I was grateful for that, I felt hopeless. How would we find you now? What if we had already missed you in the dark last night on the other side of the bridge? What if you hadn't taken this shortcut at all? What if you had gotten turned around on some other country road somewhere? Where would we even start to look for you?

I was feeling the pressure of time. You only had so much, and looking at your dad and brother's faces, I knew I wasn't the only one thinking about it. You were in real trouble if you'd been seriously injured, losing blood for who knows how long. I wouldn't let my mind go there.

Worried and disappointed, we just stood at the edge of the drop-off, watching the river rushing below, wondering what our next move would be. I started to pray quietly, asking God to show us what to do, where to go, how to find you. He had led us this far; He would lead us the rest of the way.

Just then, I heard Sandy barking. Looking back, I could see her struggling to squeeze through the partially-opened window in the back seat of the

SUV. Walking back to the vehicle, I opened the door to let her out.

Sandy darted from the SUV and broke into a run down the road. I chased after her wondering what was going on. As I ran, I prayed she was leading me to you and not just a dumb rabbit or something!

When I reached her, Sandy had stopped and was pacing back and forth at the base of a huge tree whose trunk had split partway up and fallen into the ravine below.

Stooping down, I grabbed Sandy's collar and pulled her toward me, trying to calm her, catch my breath, and look down into the ravine. Then I heard something, a faint sort of music playing. By now, your dad and John had caught up with me, anxious to see what was going on.

They heard the music, too, and your dad recognized the tune at once. "That's Grandpa's watch we're hearing! Julia has to be down there somewhere!"

I started yelling your name until we could hear you calling back to us. We followed your voice to the left until we could see your car in the ravine; it was completely covered by branches. It was hard to see, even knowing it was there! It scares me to think how easily we could've missed it without Sandy.

Never in my life had I been so relieved or happy! I knew we had a lot of work to do to get you out of there, and I didn't know how badly you might be hurt, but at least we had found my beautiful Julia. That's all I cared about at the moment. You were no longer alone.

He held me close as he finished his story; I felt so loved. With my head on his chest, I reminded him, "I wasn't alone, David. From your story, I can see my guardian angels were at work, making sure I was found in time. Damon got Sandy to the gas station, and another one—maybe Daryl—was probably making sure that nothing other than squirrels got into my car. Best of all, God Himself was there, taking care of me while I waited. He sent my man to find me, and you did. "

I could tell David was soaking in my words. He didn't speak, but by the way he held me in his arms, I knew he agreed with me.

After all that had happened, I didn't want to wait until the rehearsal dinner to give him my gift. Raising up, I asked David to hand me the jewelry box I had brought from the car. It was setting on a shelf close to where we were sitting.

Stretching to his right, David grabbed the box and passed it to me as he sat back again. I opened the box and handed him the pocket watch. After explaining its sentimental value, I asked him to read the inscription on the back.

David turned to me with tears in his eyes. "Thank you, babe. I feel the same way. I'll always treasure this watch. I love you, Julia." Then he kissed me.

For the rest of the trip back to Weston, I did something I'd been dreaming about since my accident. David moved to a captain's chair nearby, and I stretched out on the bench *completely flat!* How wonderful that felt! Before I knew it, the bride-to-be was fast asleep.

Chapter 24

Saying . . . *I do*

My dad paused outside my bedroom on his way downstairs and tapped on the door. "We need to leave in fifteen minutes, honey. You don't want to be late for your own wedding rehearsal."

"I'm almost ready," I answered back, glancing at the clock on my dresser. It was exactly five-thirty. Hurriedly, I put some finishing touches on my makeup. Looking in the mirror, it was hard to believe that only yesterday, I had been stranded in my car in the middle of nowhere, buried under a tree. After a few chiropractic adjustments and a good night's sleep, I already felt like my old self again. Tomorrow I would be marrying the man of my dreams right on schedule.

Once again, my heart flooded with gratitude for how the Lord had rescued me and preserved our wedding plans. The latest obstacles to David and I becoming man and wife had actually caused our love and appreciation for each other to deepen even more.

David's parents had already arrived from Baymont, so earlier in the day, David and I had met them for lunch. They only knew sketchy details about my accident and rescue, so we filled them in on all the particulars as we ate, including the bridge that was out just down the road from where I had crashed. The Stantons were shocked to hear how serious my accident had been. To look at me, neither of them would have guessed all I had been through. They only knew I had gone missing one day and was safely rescued the next.

"Sorry I didn't tell you more at the time, Mom and Dad. All I could think of was finding Julia. I figured we could tell you the whole story in person today."

David's parents weren't upset, just grateful I had not been seriously injured. The few scratches on my face were already starting to fade and were easily concealed by my makeup. Also, the chiropractic adjustments on my back had me pain free and standing tall.

When I arrived with my parents at the church at six o'clock, Cassie greeted me at the door with a hug and a few unexpected tears. "Sorry to be so emotional! I thought I got all this out when I saw you last night. Guess I'm still a bit shaken about almost losing my best friend. I'm so glad you're all right, Julia."

"Thanks, Cass. I love you, too. I'll try not to scare you like that again."

"Yeah, that's what you said a few years ago, after you tried to outrun that crazy guy in the middle of the night, remember?"

"Don't remind me," I said, rolling my eyes.

Our laughter was cut short when Brian walked up to us. "Pastor asked me to get you two. He wants to get started."

As Cassie and I walked toward the front of the church, I remembered an old saying: *Three times a bridesmaid, never a bride.* In my case, this proved untrue. I'd been in three weddings already, yet now it was *my* turn to be the bride.

The years of waiting had often felt long and lonely while living them, but now it all seemed a distant memory. As David and I rehearsed with our wedding party the many rituals to take place the following afternoon, we knew our love for each other had already been tested. Our marriage would be filled with many happy times and yet be strong enough to withstand a lifetime of challenges.

We had both learned to put God first and allow Him to guide us in our everyday decisions. The path ahead would not always be smooth; God never promised us that. He did, however, promise to be with us whenever the way got bumpy—to eventually bring us through every situation victoriously.

After several attempts at getting it right, Pastor Jack was finally satisfied we were all ready for tomorrow and dismissed the group. Excitement in the air, everyone headed for the country club for dinner.

Driving over, David and I were happy to have a few minutes alone together. When we got to the parking lot, David turned off the motor and pulled me close. "Tomorrow night about this time, I'll be dancing with my beautiful wife."

"And I'll be dancing with my handsome husband," I replied, beaming.

"You know, of course, every time someone clinks their glass, you have to kiss me?"

"But what if nobody does?" I teased.

"Not to worry. My groomsmen won't fail me! Maybe we should practice."

Smiling, I leaned into his embrace and received his kiss. David didn't get a second one because John was outside the car with Jenny by then, banging on the front fender. "Enough of that," he called out, laughing. "Save some kisses for tomorrow!"

The rest of the evening was filled with good food, family, and friends. During the meal, there were funny stories told and sentimental feelings expressed. When my dad prayed for David and me and our future together, his words were very touching.

Once dinner was over, I passed out gifts to my bridesmaids and to Angela, who was going to be my guest book attendant. David had something for each of his groomsmen and the four teens from the youth group who were serving as ushers.

While I unwrapped my gift from David, he took the watch I had given him out of his pocket and reread the inscription.

"Oh, David," I exclaimed, having now opened my gift. "Thank you, it's beautiful!"

"Let's see how it looks," he replied, slipping a gorgeous watch on my wrist. "Apparently, we think alike; we both chose a watch as our gift to each other."

As I was admiring the watch, Gloria walked up and handed me another box. "I have a gift for the bride, too. Only I'd rather you didn't open it here. Please wait until tomorrow after you have your wedding dress on. In my day, a bride always had to have *something old, something new, something borrowed, something blue*. This can be your *something old*."

"Thank you, Gloria. What a sweet thought! This will work out perfectly: my dress is new, I borrowed my gloves, and my garter has blue on it. The only thing I didn't have was something old."

Everyone was having such a wonderful time, no one seemed anxious to leave. But once David's dad paid the check and the staff at the country club began clearing off tables, David suggested we call it a night. I had told him earlier I wanted him to bring me home before twelve because the groom wasn't supposed to see his bride on the day of the wedding before the ceremony.

David agreed but first wanted to take a moonlight stroll with me on the pier at Murphy's Landing to reenact our first kiss out in the gazebo. This we did, amazed that very soon we would be at our wedding.

After that, David took me straight home, walked me to the doorstep, and gave me a final kiss good night. Looking into my eyes, he said, "The next time I kiss those beautiful lips of yours, we'll be married."

I sighed happily. "It doesn't seem possible that all our waiting is finally over. Tomorrow we will actually be taking our vows, and God will make us one."

David smiled at me and squeezed my hand in agreement. Checking his watch, he told me, "You'd better get inside, Cinderella; it's almost midnight."

Wishing him good night, I scooted into the house to avoid being seen after twelve. My parents were in bed already, and within fifteen minutes, so was I.

Before falling asleep, I prayed: *Thank You, Father, for giving David to me. I love him so much! In Jesus' name, help everything with our wedding to turn out perfectly tomorrow—especially my hair!*

Waking up the next morning, I realized I had slept in my house for the last time as a single woman. My parents were also aware of that fact, so my mom prepared a special breakfast for the three of us. Once we had finished eating, there wasn't time to get sentimental. My mom and I were off to the salon where Gloria and my bridesmaids were meeting us to get the works—pedicures, manicures, and fancy updos. We all had fun talking and laughing while being pampered in every way.

Fortunately, it turned out to be a good hair day for everyone. I was especially pleased with the way mine turned out. Once my veil was securely pinned in, the bridal party and mothers drove to my grandmother's house for a special luncheon.

Afterwards we rested for a bit before heading to the church to get dressed. Cassie scouted ahead to make sure David was nowhere in sight before I entered the church. When the coast was clear, I made my way down the hallway to the special dressing room used for bridal parties.

Putting on a wedding gown can be such an emotional time for a bride, with so many feelings to deal with simultaneously: happy exuberance, nervousness, and sentiments that bring tears. However, laughing or crying causes mascara to run, and that's something to be avoided at all costs!

Once I stepped into my gown, Cassie zipped it up for me. Then we stood side by side, looking into the floor-length mirror together. This was something we had done in my room hundreds of times while playing princess. Yet this time, the wedding wasn't pretend, nor the prince merely make-believe.

As I stood there, everyone in the room began to applaud me, saying over and over how beautiful I looked. And that's exactly how I felt: beautiful, valuable, and incredibly blessed to have this moment.

"Hand me that box over there, will you, Mel?" I asked, pointing to the gift box Gloria had given me the night before. Inside was a note and the most stunning teardrop diamond earrings I'd ever seen. I removed the note and silently read it:

Daughter,
These earrings were a gift from my father to my
mother to wear on her wedding day. She passed
them down to me when I married Bill, and now

*I'm passing them on to you. One day, perhaps your
daughter will wear them.
All my love,
Mother Stanton*

I was deeply touched and, looking across the
room at Gloria, could only mouth the words *thank you*
as I fought to hold back tears. Seeing I was about to
cry, Jenny quickly handed me some tissues, warning,
"No, no, no—your nose will swell!" Everyone started
laughing, including me. Carefully, I removed the earrings I was wearing and inserted the much better
choice.

Glancing over, I saw Cassie struggling a bit to
get into her own dress. It seemed her waist had
expanded a little since her last fitting, but for good
reason: she and Brian were expecting their first baby.
Jenny hurried over to help her with the zipper.

Meanwhile, my mom checked her watch. "It's
time," she announced. "We need to get lined up."

As I stood in the back of the church, waiting as
the mothers lit candles up front, I held tightly to my
father's arm. Looking up at him, I was aware that
after he walked me down the aisle, our relationship
would be forever changed; an important exchange
was about to take place at the altar. Once he placed
my hand into David's, my dad would no longer be
responsible to God for my care and protection. That
job would be transferred to David.

At that moment, as though he were reading my
thoughts, my dad looked down at me, took a deep

breath, and affectionately patted my hand, too overcome with emotion to speak.

The processional music snapped both of us out of our reflections, and Melody led the way for the bridesmaids. Of course, when it was their turn, Magda, dressed as a miniature bride, and John Jr., smartly clad in a tiny tuxedo, momentarily stole the show during their adorable journey down the aisle. Once they were received by my mother and seated next to my grandparents, the congregation was asked to stand. The bridal march began to play.

Fixing his eyes straight ahead, David watched me slowly walking toward him. His smile told me I was the most beautiful bride he had ever seen.

When my father and I arrived at the altar, Pastor Jack asked, "Who gives this woman to be married to this man?" Once my dad responded, he lifted my veil enough to kiss me goodbye. Then he reached for my hand, confidently placed it into David's, and took his seat beside my mother.

By now, David and I were looking into each other's eyes, radiating with happiness. As we turned to face the pastor, ready to take our vows, both of us silently thanked the Lord for bringing us together.

The ceremony continued flawlessly, just as we'd hoped. Once David and I finished saying *I do* to the traditional vows made in every wedding ceremony, we spoke some special words we had prepared and memorized to say to each other.

Though each of us expressed it differently, the message was the same: The love we felt for each other was a gift from God—one that was meant to last a lifetime. Our ability to keep our vows would require constant devotion to Christ as the center of our marriage; He was the glue necessary to both join us as one and keep us together for life.

Next, we took communion together for the first time as man and wife, giving a rose to each of our parents afterward. In closing, Pastor Jack charged us with the seriousness of the vows we had just made to one another. Breaking into a smile, he instructed David, "You may now kiss your bride."

David turned toward me and carefully lifted my veil, meeting my gaze as he smoothed out the netting around my shoulders. He paused ever so slightly and smiled before leaning down and kissing me the way every woman wants to be kissed by the man she loves. For an instant, we were the only two people on earth. When our lips parted, Pastor Jack's voice brought us back to reality. "May I present to you for the very first time: Mr. and Mrs. David Stanton."

As applause from the congregation rose, the recessional music began, and we led the bridal party out of the sanctuary. David and I returned shortly to dismiss our guests row by row, receiving their congratulations. With such a late afternoon ceremony, there was just enough time for pictures before leaving for the reception.

For the next hour, both the photographer and videographer worked hard recording lasting memories of our wedding day. When the session in the sanctuary was over, David and I expected to leave for the reception in a limousine. An unexpected surprise awaited us outside: a beautiful open carriage with four white horses stood ready to take us to the Weston Inn, an added gift from David's parents.

We climbed aboard with Brian and Cassie and rode through the downtown area, receiving smiles and waves from almost every passerby. My heart was nearly bursting with joy as I sat beside my amazing husband, savoring each moment of our special day.

Right on schedule, the carriage arrived at the reception hall, and our fairy tale continued. The rest of the evening was spent visiting with family and friends, eating a delicious dinner, and dancing.

Every tradition was tastefully observed: toasts to the bride and groom, special dances between family members, the cutting of the cake, and the throwing of the bridal bouquet.

I was especially pleased that my friends from Tyler University were able to attend our wedding. When I sent the invitations out, I hadn't expected Karen and her husband, Matt, to make it since they were missionaries in Spain. On her response card, Karen explained it would work out because they were already coming home on furlough.

Gary and Gretchen had asked their parents to watch their kids, leaving early that morning to get to the ceremony on time.

Even Kenny showed up—with a guest. At last, God had brought him the woman he'd been searching for. Meeting her, I felt sure he was more than happy he'd waited so long for her; she was smart, fun, and pretty, too.

David enjoyed meeting my former rescue squad, and I loved showing off my wonderful husband. I purposely arranged for my friends to sit together at the same table so it would be easier for me to talk to all of them and catch up on their lives. It was great seeing them again.

Amidst all the activity, David managed to steal me away for some romantic moments under the stars on the outside patio overlooking the lake. There we danced to a special song he had requested.

As previously instructed, John found us dancing outdoors and reminded David that he wanted to leave by ten o'clock. Once our departure was announced, we said private farewells to our parents, grandparents, and each member of the wedding party. As I gave Cassie a final hug, I whispered in her ear, "Now it's your turn to pray for me!"

Changing into traveling clothes, we walked out of the building to where Flip had a limo waiting for us. The remaining guests met us outside and released a shower of bubbles as we slid inside the limo. Before we drove away, John and Jenny poked their heads inside to give us a final farewell and to assure David they would take good care of Sandy while we were gone.

Our plans to spend our honeymoon in Hawaii would be slightly delayed. David wanted us to spend some time together before having to travel. So he reserved a suite at a hotel near the airport to allow us time for a leisurely breakfast before boarding our plane at noon the next day.

As we neared the hotel, David looked over at me and squeezed my hand. "Can you believe we're married?"

I blushed a little. "Yes, but I am a little nervous."

"Me, too, but it's a nice kind of nervous. All we have to do is relax, take it slow, and let the love we have for each other guide us. Here we are," he added as the limo driver pulled up to the entrance.

It felt funny to be checking into a hotel with David. Since we were getting the bridal suite, it was no secret we were newlyweds.

"Can I get you anything else?" the bellhop asked after placing our luggage in the room.

"No thanks," David responded, reaching into his pocket to pass him a tip. After the bellhop left, David returned to where he had asked me to wait in the hallway.

"Now, Mrs. Stanton, it's time for the groom to carry the bride across the threshold."

Instantly, he swept me up into his arms and carried me inside. Setting me down, he drew me in close and kissed me. For the next few minutes, we toured the luxurious suite together hand in hand. Then, while I was changing in the bathroom, David placed a *Do Not Disturb* sign outside our door so we wouldn't be interrupted.

We had honored God by remaining virgins during our whole courtship and engagement. Now that we were finally man and wife, we were both more than ready to exchange an incredibly precious, one-time gift.

Epilogue

As you read this book, did you think about your own spiritual life? Did you already know that God loves you and wants to be close to you—or did the relationship that Julia and her friends had with God seem strange or unattainable? Maybe no one has told you how much you mean to God.

The Bible says in John 3:16-18: *God loved the world so very, very much that He gave His only Son. Because He did that, everyone who believes in Him will not lose his life, but will live forever. God did not send His Son in the world to judge the world. He sent Him to save the world. Everyone who believes in the Son will not be judged. But everyone who does not believe in Him is judged already, because he does not believe in the name of God's only Son.* (Worldwide English Version).©

These verses tell us that God wants *everyone* to be in His family. Yet not everyone will be. We are all born with a sinful nature that separates us from a holy God—and a sin debt that is too great for anyone to pay. That's why Jesus paid that debt for us on the cross. He paid what we could not. And now we have access to God the Father once again. All that remains is our choice to accept or reject His offer of salvation.

So, if you have never accepted Jesus as your Savior and Lord, you have a decision to make. Ask your-self: *Do I want to run my own life, miss heaven, and*

*experience less than God's best for me right now? Or
do I want to receive what Christ did for me and allow
God to direct my life from this day forward, letting Him
heal my past hurts and design a better future for me?*
This choice is yours to make.

If you've already given your life to Jesus and
received Him as *Savior*, you have His promise of
eternal life in heaven. But it is important to make
Christ the *Lord* of your life as well. When Jesus is your
Lord, you seek God's will for your life, taking the time
to pray, read the Bible, and then do what He tells you
(to the best of your ability). As you honor God in this
way, you will remain under the protective umbrella of
His truth and provision. And you will experience the
abundant blessings that come through simple faith,
trust, and obedience. If you resist this part, however,
you will miss out on much of God's best for your life.

How to Receive Jesus as Savior and Lord

If you have never given your life to the Lord but
would like to, He is ready and willing to receive you.
If you will pray this prayer from your heart, He will
give you a new heart that wants to love and serve
Him.

*Heavenly Father, I come to you in Jesus' name and
ask You to forgive me for the things I have done
wrong and for wanting to live life my own way.
Right now I invite Jesus to come into my heart and
take control of my life. I believe that He died on the
cross to pay for my sins: past, present and future.
I believe that He was raised from the dead and*

will welcome me in heaven when my earthly life is over. Please help me to live for You and for others. I believe You have heard my prayer and that I have been born of Your Spirit. I confess Jesus as my Lord and Savior, and I am now a Christian, one who follows Christ.

If you have prayed this prayer for the first time or are rededicating your life to the Lord, you need to find a church that teaches the Bible and will help you grow in your relationship with God. You won't be able to reach your full potential without the help of other Christians.

The best way to know God for yourself is to set aside time to study your Bible and pray. Journaling is another way to connect with God as you record your thoughts and prayers. Over time you can see how you've grown and how God continues to take care of you.

From the Authors

Marrying Mr. Right is the third novel in the **MR. RIGHT SERIES**. We hope you have enjoyed taking this journey with Julia Duncan from her college years until she finally meets and marries the man of her dreams.

As you shared Julia's adventures in this book, how did you relate to her? Would you have been able to forgive Professor McNulty and Gloria Stanton the way she did? Do you think you would have had the courage to halt your engagement like Julia, trusting God to make a way where there seemed to be no solution? How would you have spent your time waiting to be rescued if you were in a similar accident? Is your trust in God and His Word strong enough to bring you through challenging trials?

During the years of waiting for her Mr. Right, Julia spent her time developing an intimate relationship with God. It was her unwavering trust in Him and His promises that helped her stay strong and continue to believe in the midst of difficult problems that threatened to steal her happiness.

Our prayer is that the practical truths woven throughout Julia's story will help you learn from what she experienced, to remind you to protect yourself from all the Mr. Wrongs out there who will try to take advantage of you.

The central theme of this series is the central theme of the Bible: God loves you and wants the very best for your life. The only one who can keep you from tapping into His blessings, however, is *you*, by making foolish choices.

As a young woman, I (Barbara) learned just how costly wrong choices can be; my life seemed shipwrecked by the time I was twenty years old. After experiencing a painful divorce at such a young age, I thankfully turned the management of my life over to the Lord, and I've been on a new and better path ever since.

Truthfully, we don't have the wisdom to govern our own lives any more than we have the perfection to earn our way into heaven. That's why we need to surrender our hearts to God as both our Savior and our Lord. Once we understand that He means only to bless and mature us, surrendering to Him becomes a joy.

Try to remember that the enemy of your soul wants to keep you from experiencing a happy marriage. But if you refuse to get impatient, God will hold your hand while you're *waiting for Mr. Right*, will schedule a time and place for *meeting Mr. Right*, and will shower you with abundant blessings when you're finally *marrying Mr. Right*.

We pray our readers will hear their Heavenly Father's heart calling to them from each page in the series, that they will come to understand just how much He loves them, and allow Him to protect them and provide a blessed future for them.

The **MR. RIGHT SERIES** has been well worth our years of labor since it allows us to mentor more girls corporately than we ever could have individually. This work is lovingly written to inspire and encourage all the daughters within the Christian faith. Some we already know and love, others we have yet to meet, and some we will never know personally until heaven one day.

Our heartfelt prayer for each of you is best expressed in a few lines taken from a song in the musical *Fiddler on the Roof*. Tevye and Golde sang it to their daughters on the Sabbath:

> *May you be like Ruth and like Esther,*
> *May you be deserving of praise,*
> *Strengthen them, Oh Lord,*
> *And keep them from the stranger's ways.*

Don't miss any part of Julia's continuing story! The other two novels in the Mr. Right Series are available now.

Who do you know that would love to read this book?

Captivating! I began reading this morning at 7 a.m. and could not put the book down! My mind was reeling with the names of all the people I must tell about this book.

Barbara Rush-Businesswoman

The Mr. Right Novel Series

ISBN: 978-1-60683-493-0
Trade Paper, 176 pages

Novel #1
Waiting for Mr. Right
Written by Lisa Raftery and Barbara Precourt

In the first installment of the series, you will meet Julia as she enters her first year of college. It's an exciting time, but she quickly learns that life away from her traditional Christian home is different. In fact, she finds herself compromising her values to try and fit in. One lie leads to another, putting her very life in danger. Although Julia dreams of the day she will walk down the aisle with her Mr. Right, she's got to survive dating first!

ISBN: 978-1-60683-494-7
Trade Paper, 304 pages

Novel #2
Meeting Mr. Right
Written by Lisa Raftery and Barbara Precourt

After a traumatic first year of college, Julia is back in her hometown. She learned the hard way the dangers of dating Mr. Wrong and has put her priorities back on track, determined this time to wait for the right guy. Julia wants to do the right thing, but there's a new set of temptations that await. Can Julia's relationship with God help her make better choices?

Available now at www.HarrisonHouse.com
and other bookstores nationwide